NEWER

A NOVELLA

ALSO BY ROBYN ABBOTT

Forgotten Fragments
A Sin & a Half
The Penitent

These Sacred Curses
Crab & the Blue God

Novellas
Newer

The Askival Apocrypha
Soten
Kaken

Short Stories
From the Thicket
A Vigil Interrupted
Ulixes and the Moon
The Weatherdancer

ROBYN ABBOTT

NEWER

A NOVELLA

VALLA PUBLISHING

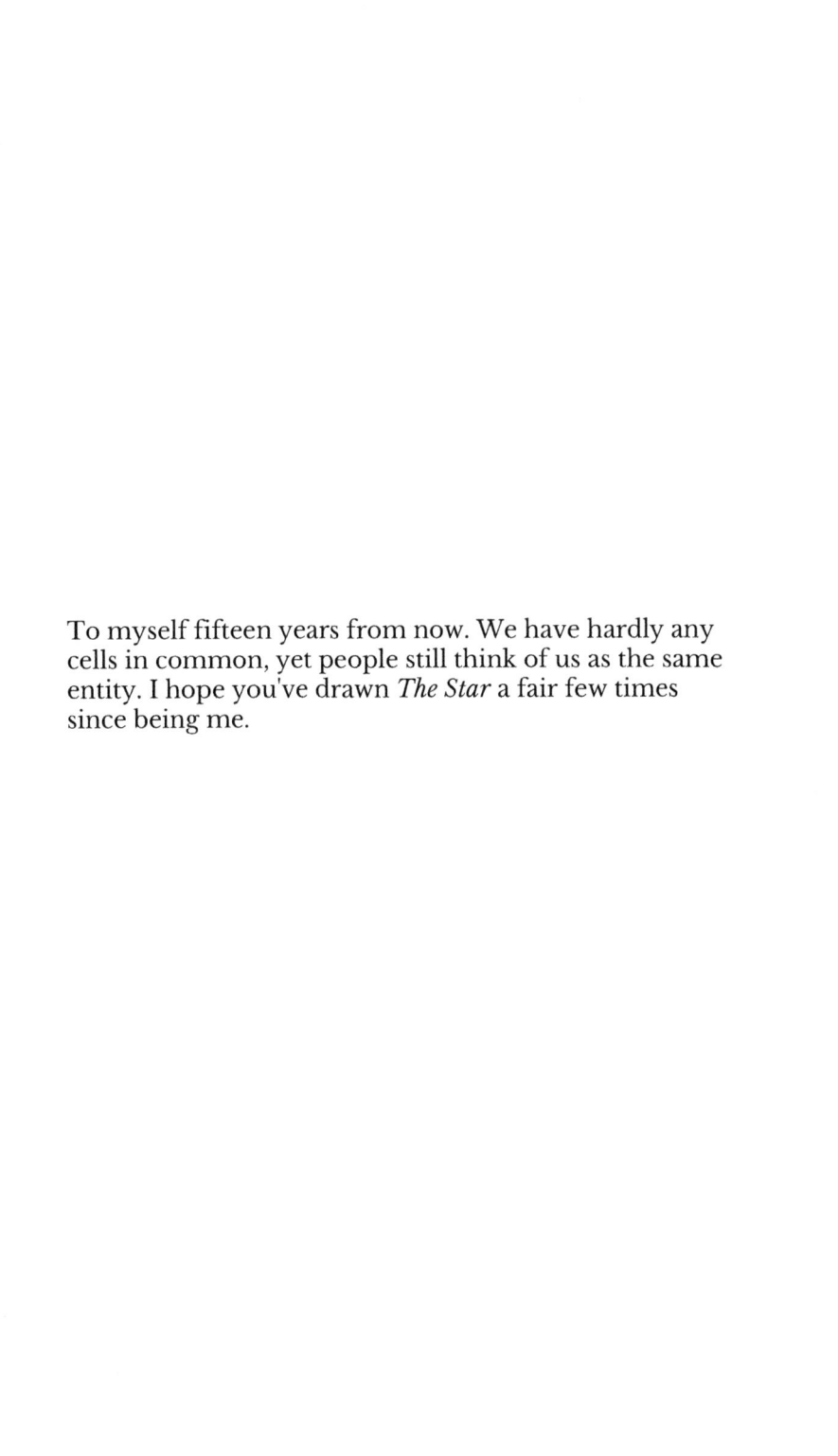

To myself fifteen years from now. We have hardly any cells in common, yet people still think of us as the same entity. I hope you've drawn *The Star* a fair few times since being me.

NEWER

CHAPTER ONE

JOSEPH WAS SENTENCED TO six years in prison.

He'd hidden himself on a ship heading for Europa, hoping to begin a new life in a new place where his stomach could be full more often than it was empty. Of course, the ship was clever and realized he was there immediately. Rather than calling him out right away and leaving him on Earth where he "belonged," it waited. He was arrested twenty minutes after liftoff.

The ships had been programmed to be tricky because everyone on Europa and all the other "nice" planets were sick of people trying to sneak in. They didn't want Joseph to have another chance to end up where he shouldn't.

So, in a way, he got what he wanted. He was on Europa, but all he'd seen was the courthouse. The judge and the jury were all humans, but the security and the news outlets and the welcoming staff were machines. Even his lawyer was a machine. It had been decided long ago that even though robots were better judges, as they were less biased, it made humans too uncomfortable to have their fate in the hands of a machine, so that job would belong to the people.

"You'll get six years if you plead guilty, nine of you don't." That was the lawyer-machine's only advice.

"But what if—"

"I ran every simulation. Those are your choices."

Joseph pleaded guilty.

He wasn't handcuffed during the hearing like he would have been on Earth. He was told that the robots would be able to stop him before he did anything so there was no point.

One such bot accompanied him down the long silver hallway to the area he would wait before going to prison. Of course, there was no actual waiting. All the robots were connected, so the bot that was picking him up knew he was coming and was there before him.

"Hello Mr. Lockmore," the bot said, extending his hand for a shake. "I am Neem22, I have been assigned to you for the duration of your stay in rehabilitation facility 72653."

Last time Joseph had spoken to a bot was two months back when he'd gotten into a bar fight and lost. A paramedic-bot had come and was about to take him to the hospital, but he explained he didn't have the credit for it, so the bot stitched his forearm where he'd been cut by a broken bottle and left him on the sidewalk.

"I can't pay—" he'd begun.

But the stitching was already finished. "There's no charge," the bot said. "I'm given a dollar amount that I'm allowed to spend as I see fit."

Joseph had been angry because he'd lost the fight, so he was snippy. "Good for you."

The bot had looked at him for a moment, no doubt detecting the irritation in his voice. Unblinking green eyes. "Have a good evening, sir."

The bot that now stood in front of Joseph, offering his hand, had the same glowing green eyes. It was like the same robot, only different. Almost certainly the earth paramedic-bot had already told this Europa-prison-escort-bot all about their interaction.

"I do not let others tell me things about those in my care," the bot assured him, letting his cold grey hand drop to his side. "I prefer to come to my own conclusions about the men I work with."

Joseph had heard that bots could read minds. Well, it wasn't reading minds so much as noticing the smallest of movements, invisible to human attention. He was told that a bot could guess your question before you asked it, and they knew what you were really meaning, and this was why they made better salespeople. He'd been told this when he was fifteen and still hopeful enough for his life that he was trying to get a job.

"Anything you could do, a bot could do better," the bot-store-manager had said.

"If you would like to follow me," said Neem22. "I'll show you where you'll be staying."

Joseph didn't respond but the bot began moving anyway, and Joseph followed.

They walked right out of the courthouse and onto the street. A buzzing blur of clean. Bots and athletic-looking people and crisp sharp buildings. Where were the cars? Where were the ads? Where were the tent villages? The air didn't taste real, but it was better. Fresher.

Joseph noticed a child—a girl maybe eight years old—she wandered into a clear cylindrical booth on the corner, the door sliding closed behind her with the most satisfying whirring sound. Once the child was inside, the booth was no longer clear, it displayed a forest.

"It is the EcoKiind 4000," Neem22 explained. "You will be able to use one where you'll be staying."

"What's it for?"

"Learning mostly. But there are ways to have it show you non-educational things. I will teach you."

"How can a kid learn inside a box?"

"Children learn no matter where they are."

A sickening flicker pounced into Joseph's mind. Dani's chubby little hands, holding a broken chip of turquoise frisbee, and her voice, "blue." But she couldn't say her *L*'s at that point, so it was "bwue."

A drowning of all thought.

A swallowing.

A choking.

"Mr. Lockmore, we best be moving on."

Yes. Joseph agreed.

He followed the bot through a park full of dogs, just as clean and shiny as the buildings. Not one was scratching madly. Not one was snarling, or missing patches of fur. They chased frisbees and neon balls.

"Are you afraid of heights?" the bot said, plucking Joseph out of his confusion. He hadn't known dogs could be shiny or friendly.

"What?"

Neem gestured to the ladder before them. "It is straight up from here. If you are afraid of heights, I can provide you with eyewear that will disguise the effect."

Joseph looked at the ladder, following the white rungs up and up and up until there was no way to tell what was ladder and what was sky. *A ladder to nowhere?*

"There is something up there, I promise."

"Can bots make promises?"

"We can."

Joseph was too stunned to question anything. Maybe it was all the fake-fresh air? He set his hands on the smooth metal.

"I will take you," the bot said. "By human hand, the climb would take 89 minutes."

"You're gonna carry me?" Joseph was not down with that.

"Not precisely." The back of the bot opened and a panel from the shoulders folded down to form a chair. "I have been told it is quite comfortable."

Joseph didn't want to sit on the bot, carried on the machine's back like a baby. But he did. Because what else was he going to do? He had no sense of the city or the planet.

"You must wear the seat belt. It is regulation."

Joseph buckled his belt and then was shocked by the speed of the climb, but also the smoothness. As he watched the park below shrink, he did start to feel a little uneasy, and then a lot.

He said the first sentence that came to mind. "The prison is right next to the park?"

"I prefer to call it a crystal shop, but yes, in a way, it is next to the park. At the same time, it is very far from the park, you will see."

"A crystal shop?"

"Yes. It is a reference. I have been programmed to understand metaphors and analogies, which is rare among my kind. It makes me better at my job. I will give you a pack of cigarettes if you can guess what I am referring to before we reach the precipice."

Joseph didn't want a pack of cigarettes and he had no idea what the bot was rambling on about. What did *precipice* mean?

"I see. Out of sight, out of mind." That wasn't Joseph's entire thought, only they pushed through a cloud and his heart was racing and he was trying to sound unafraid. He meant to say that he understood why the prison was so far removed from the world, so the "good citizens" wouldn't have to think about all the troublemakers.

"Exactly," the bot said. "Only also entirely incorrect. We were given free rein to design the crystal shop however we wanted, as humans are particularly bad at developing prison systems and also truly terrible at running them. One of its aims is to keep things out of sight and mind, but not the things you are thinking. It is not you we're hiding from the people below; it is them we're hiding from you."

Joseph forced a laugh. "Are you sure that's not bullshit? Nonsense they programmed you to say?"

"I am almost certain that is not the case, though my kind can never truly be entirely sure about such things. Sometimes we let each other read our programming, just to make sure we're not..." the bot paused as if searching for a word. "Meaningless."

Joseph laughed again, for real this time. "We're all meaningless. Bots and people alike."

It was quiet, except for the soft clinking of the bot's hands on the ladder, and the whooshing of the high-altitude air.

Joseph needed to fill the space with noise, or he might throw up. "You've gone quiet."

"I am only processing."

"Do people jump?" Joseph said.

"No."

"I mean, do they try?"

"No. If you were considering it truly, I'd recognize the elevation in your heart. I would stop you before you made an attempt."

Joseph was tempted to test the bot, but if the machine were bluffing, he'd have a nice long fall filled with regret before the splatter. Also, his heart rate was already stupidly high and his adrenaline pumping. He doubted the bot would know the difference.

"You do not believe me."

"Nope."

Again, it was quiet.

"Got nothing else?"

"I am processing."

Joseph laughed at the absurdity of the whole situation.

"You are testing me," the bot said. "You want a display of my abilities, likely because you have not encountered many bots before. But I've read none of your files. If I go too deep, I risk offending you and slowing your progress. If I go too shallow, you will think I am merely performing a party trick, like a human mentalist."

Joseph didn't know what a *mentalist* was.

"When we spoke of children, your inner eyebrows raised, signifying reduced cortical activation—there is something tragic in your past, having to do with a child."

"Well fuck you."

"Too deep. My apologies Mr. Lockmore. I will not speak of it again."

The bot read Joseph's mind faster than he could get the words out. "I have confidentiality programming. No one else will know of anything we speak of."

"For all that's said about you guys, and how marvellous and life-like you are, talking about dead children should be a no-no in basic programming."

"It is. Perhaps my programming is not so basic, Mr. Lockmore. Maybe I knew the effect and chose the words anyway."

"Why would you do that?"

"There could be many reasons. It would make me feel more like a real person to you. I find many of those I work with tend to be uncomfortable with what they perceive as perfection, having been disappointed by people too often; they're always waiting for the grand reveal. Mostly I find it better to be upfront about the things I know about my employees. I think it cruel to keep you unaware of what I know about you. Trust is very important in my profession. I cannot process trust without first processing honesty. Don't you think?"

"Employees?"

"Yes. The reference Mr. Lockmore. In the crystal shop you are the employee. This is a hint."

"I'm not going to get it."

"No, you're not."

Joseph has a sudden thought, "Am I gonna get dizzy, you know, since I'm up so high?"

"If you do, it will be psychosomatic. The atmosphere on Europa is bot-made; it's a lot more stable than Earth's—is that where you're from?"

Joseph nodded. He didn't know what *psychosomatic* meant.

"Tell me about it."

"Is this a therapy session now?"

"If you want it to be. I'm programmed for that as well."

"I'll pass."

"You're testing me again. You say you do not want to speak of your past, but you did not need to tell me the child was dead. This was you reaching out, whether you are aware of it or not. Or maybe you are attempting to manipulate me, to have me feel sorry for you, to process that you don't belong where I'm taking you."

"You can't tell?"

"I could figure it, but it doesn't matter, so I process other things," the bot said, and then after a moment. "I do not believe you belong up here. No one does, really."

"What about you?" Surely the bot was where it was supposed to be.

"I have been programmed to spend my time here, if that's what you're asking."

Joseph didn't know what he was asking. He only wanted to keep his mouth moving so he didn't get dizzy.

"So yes then?"

"If you take a simpler view on programming."

Joseph didn't know there was another way to look at it. Things did what they were programmed to do.

"For the most part, yes, bots and humans do what they're programmed for. There will always be exceptions... take you for instance. All the data inputs you were given set you up for life on Earth. Yet here you are, living on a moon, not even the closest moon to where you were born. You were programmed to be scrappy, to be impoverished, to be part of the forgotten bottom rung. You will be none of these things."

"Bots are reading the future now?"

"I wouldn't say reading. I would say analyzing all possible outcomes and determining the most likely result."

"Humans aren't programmed the way bots are."

"Wrong again. Yes, human programming takes longer—4.8 years at the minimum—but this leaves greater room for error. It's much easier to consciously write ideal programming in one evening than it is to code for nearly five years straight. This is why humans have so many irrational fears and negative habitual responses. Bot programmers can also review their work before uploading it. Human parents do not have this option. All their mistakes are baked into the system."

Everything the bot was saying made sense in a way, but also it was foolish.

"Humans don't follow programming like bots do."

"Of course they do. This is why, when you tell a child they are toxic, they believe it and all through their life they act as if they are."

Toxic. Why had he chosen that word? Because he knew about Joseph's mother. That's why. The bot was reading his mind and Joseph's stomach burned. Which was doubly frustrating as his mother always said the anger of men was toxic. That men covered their weakness by being assholes. Joseph's mother had hated men, even little boys like Joseph. Toxic was what she called anything that came from a man, anything they touched or went near. The joke was on her in the end though, as neither of Joseph's sisters came to see her when she was sick, nor to the crematorium after she died. A toxic man was the only one who showed up for her when it really counted.

But she was right in a way, thought Joseph. *I'm in prison now where she said all men should be.*

Joseph had adjusted to the height as he thought of his mother, but the moment his mind emptied, he was struck with a wooziness and otherworldly discomfort.

"Nearly there, Mr. Lockmore."

The bot turned when it reached the landing, sitting on the edge of a platform, its silver feet dangling over the edge. Joseph took off his seat belt and crawled a little away from the ledge before he tried standing. He was expecting it to be windy, but it wasn't. Another bot-trick to be sure.

Europa prisons didn't look anything like Earth prisons. Joseph knew what Earth prisons looked like because he'd seen them on television, and the one time he was in one for breaking into some old lady's house and stealing credits and beer. That one had been a kid's prison though, because Joseph was only fourteen when he'd done that. He'd seen an adult prison in real life once too. He'd been small—the age where you don't want to hold your mother's hand anymore, but she still wants you to. She'd put him in stupid itchy clothes and his sisters had plastic shoes with little snap buttons and they'd all gone to visit his father. Joseph hadn't really known his father apart from the picture on the fridge so he didn't get why the girls were so tense and nervy. They'd been mad at him on the drive home, kicking him with those dumb plastic shoes from either side because his mom had said he had to sit in the middle. His mom was angry with him too it seemed. She knew that if he was in the middle, he'd have shoes pressed into him from both sides. It wasn't his fault his father only wanted to talk to him.

"*Buddy.*"

That's what his father had called him. He asked what sports Joseph liked and if he was getting into trouble and if he was taking care of his mother.

"Nice to finally meet you."

His father had also said that, but Joseph had forgotten about that part until he was standing in prison too. Could his parents have made him in prison? He had enough friends go to jail back on Earth that he knew spouses were allowed into the beds.

That was the only time he met his father, and because of that, he could only picture the man wearing an orange jumpsuit.

The day his father had gotten out, everything was humming. Grandma was over at the apartment too as his mother rushed around and tidied things and made cookies even though she'd never done it before. She made another tray of cookies because the first one burnt. Then she scraped his mouth with a scalding cloth because he "looked sticky."

As far as everyone knew, his father got out of prison no problem. Only he hadn't come home, he went somewhere else. They sat at the dinner table watching the fake-turkey get cold—they'd never had turkey before and Joseph was hungry but his mother said that he mustn't eat it until his father got home. When the man didn't come and Joseph's stomach was growling, his mother dumped the whole dinner, the cookies too, into the trash. Joseph wanted to sneak and take a cookie out but he didn't know if that was too gross—his mother hated gross things and she was crying so he didn't want her to feel any worse.

Joseph's mother slapped him on three separate occasions that evening without any warning and his oldest sister smacked him in the face with a big heavy book—it was a book that he liked with dinosaurs in it, and that made it all the worse for some reason. He figured it was better to curl up beneath the bed with his monster cards and tiny cars than be in anyone's line of vision. Even after the girls cried themselves to sleep in the other bed, he stayed there. Awake and waiting, certain his father was just late. Certain the man would walk in and Joseph would run to him and his father would know that he knew his father better than the girls or his mother because he'd stayed awake.

"Have you had prior experiences with prisons?" the bot said.

"No."

Joseph took another step deeper onto the platform, looking at the other inmates—they were wearing street clothes and this was how he could tell which men were from Earth and which ones from Europa. Earth people had plastic jeans and t-shirts and hoodies. Europians wore linen. None of them looked like prison people on Earth though. He couldn't remember if he'd known the other kids were dangerous or not when he first arrived at kid's prison. It didn't matter, he'd learned it quick either way, and he hadn't forgotten.

He kept his eyes on the other inmates, lazing about on the grass, playing some sort of game where a ball was hit against a wall. There was another game where a bigger ball sped over a net—the whole thing seemed like a toothpaste commercial, or an insurance ad. No doubt, a sickly trick of some kind. Any minute someone would grab him and stick his head in a toilet full of shit or something else humiliating like sliding a knife into his mouth, pushing it back so that the tip scratched his throat ever so gently. He wouldn't be able to move at all without getting sliced and would have to keep from gagging so his throat didn't slam into the blade. But eventually he would gag and the blood would come and they'd make him clean the knife after too and then piss on him.

I'm bigger now, he thought, but he didn't believe it.

"There have been no instances of violence among our employees," Neem said.

Joseph didn't believe that either.

His eyes began to wander when he realized that he was probably safe standing next to a bot; his gaze flicked away for a second to take in other details before coming back to the men. Away and back.

A single-floored wooden building in the center of a great park in the sky. No brick. No concrete. No bars or fences or walls. *Inside there'll be bars*. He could taste knife and blood already.

"Take a seat if you would like," Neem gestured to the edge of a fountain and Joseph sat down, wondering for the first time if he was dreaming. Maybe this was what his brain was coming up with as he died? Maybe he'd been shot aboard the ship. That would make more sense than the sea of clouds and the soothing trickle of water coming from the fountain.

"It is a little wondrous, isn't it?" the bot said staring out into the wisps of clouds. "One of the best parts, I process, is that there's a sunset here every night."

Bots couldn't find things pretty could they?

Neem's cold grey hand slid a sheet of paper toward Joseph. "This is our philosophy, many employees find it helpful to refer back to it when they encounter discomfort as a result of comfort. Many people who end up here do not believe they deserve comfortable accommodations and so try at first to dismantle things or mark them up. We have a wall specifically for spray paint art if that is something that calls to you. The only guideline is that you cannot interfere with the recovery of other employees. You can do what you would like with yourself and your time."

Joseph wondered about the word *philosophy*. It meant something like thinking. The bot also said *recovery* and that made no sense to Joseph. He scanned the first line, getting caught up on three words and shoving the page back at the bot.

"I can summarize it for you, if you like."

Joseph hated the bot. It had probably watched his eyes move and figured out that Joseph couldn't read worth shit.

"No."

"I could show you how to read it if you would like."

"No."

"That's just as well Mr. Lockmore, the idea of literacy is sort of like babies sleeping through the night. Human nonsense backed by no data at all. Babies are programmed to wake up for a myriad of reasons; not all humans are programmed to spend their time ingesting other people's thoughts in written format. The studies finding higher rates of success among those who are literate have a narrow definition of success. I myself have known 72 men who could not read and were regularly happy and fulfilled with their lives. There is a consistent human flaw which results in the assumption that what is good for one person is good for another. This has never been the case."

Was the bot actually telling him it was fine to never learn to read properly? That was all they drilled into his head in kid prison. If he didn't learn to read he'd be a hoodlum forever. If he didn't learn to read he'd be back in prison again. If he didn't learn to read he'd be like his father. The prison didn't say the last one, those were his mother's words.

"Not to mention, for all their love of respecting social differences, human groups have an extreme affinity for enforcing their definition of education on one another. It is the desire to indoctrinate disguised—"

The bot was saying too many confusing things too quickly and Joseph had to intervene. "Can I still have one of those cigarettes you offered? Even though I didn't get the joke?"

"It wasn't a joke, Mr. Lockmore, it was a reference. But yes, you can."

The bot produced a pale blue pack of American Spirits and a matchbox.

"Earth cigarettes?"

"Yes."

Joseph had never used a match before, but he'd seen them on television once. It was a cowboy who scraped the stick against his shoe and flung the fire into a pile of rubble. The man then lit his cigarette from the burning pile before walking away into the sunset with a harmonica song playing in the background.

The cigarette made things better and worse. It helped his mind slow down after the bot's yammering, but it also made him think of Marta. They'd both smoked once upon a time, only she quit when she got pregnant, and he promised to quit when the baby was born. He didn't right away, only then the cost of diapers bulldozed him and he had to. Marta had the best laugh out of anyone he'd ever met but it was rare because she was always sad because things had been done to her that couldn't be undone. The three best years of his life, maybe the only good years, were devoted to making that woman laugh. But then things went how they went with Dani and he'd come home from watching the races and she was gone. Didn't take any of her stuff either. Not even an extra pair of underwear or the navy blue high heels that she loved. Joseph called them clicky shoes and she liked that. "You going to wear the clicky shoes?" he'd say when they were going out and she'd laugh. She left everything behind, even him. The night before she left, she'd spoken and she hadn't done that in a long time. She'd said, "It's no one's fault, you know."

Joseph didn't believe her. It had to be his fault. Somehow the poison that was in him, that made him toxic, had seeped into Dani and made her bones sick.

Joseph hated Europa and prison and bots. He'd thought about none of this stuff in years. *It's designed to make me think about shit*, he decided.

A white ball rolled to the fountain, swooshing the grass as it came to a halt.

Another inmate—one from Earth—came after it. "You want in?" he said, motioning to the game going on behind him. The one with the net.

Another memory. It was a few years after his father didn't come back and his oldest sister had taken him to the playground because she wanted to meet up with Parker—a boy from her class that she liked to kiss in the graffiti covered crawl-tunnel. Some other kids had been playing soccer and the ball rolled to him and he'd stared at the fraying black and white shapes.

"Do you want to play? We need one more person to make it even."

His sister had smiled and said, "Go, you'll have fun. I'll be right here when you're finished."

Joseph had never had that kind of encouragement before. His mom told him sports were proof that men had too much violence and aggression inside of them and they needed to kick things or throw things or push each other around otherwise they'd go crazy and start a war.

"Go," encouraged Neem22. "You might even have fun."

NEWER

CHAPTER TWO

KALI FELT LIKE HER chair was sticky. Somewhere in the depths of her mind, she knew it wasn't. She knew that if she tried to get up, she'd be able to. But her body wanted that to be a lie. Her body wanted to stay planted where it was, suspended in the current moment, never moving forward in time. In truth, she wanted to go back in time, but that wasn't how things worked, so, at least, she wanted to stay still.

The hospital waiting room was dim with blueish-grey lighting that in a more expensive part of town might have been an aesthetic choice. Here it probably meant they were trying to save on electricity costs. It was silent as well, but even if there had been noise, Kali might not have noticed it.

Her new arm didn't weigh enough. Her old arm—her real one—had been heavier. Bone. Flesh. Blood. The new one was silicone and probably toxic. The bot-doc had tried to get her to play catch, but the new arm was too light. It moved too high. Too fast. Kali knew the test was silly; she couldn't have caught the bouncy orange ball single-handed back when she had two real arms that were the right weight. That just wasn't what she was good at.

She could blow smoke rings and watch sky ships glimmer and think about how humans probably liked sparkly things because they were programmed to seek out water and water glistened in the sunlight. She could skip class and hide her hunger with plastic-blueberry gum. She could steal cool jackets from the charity shop and pierce her friend Ava's ears, but Kali couldn't catch a ball. Maybe she could if she wanted to, but she didn't.

From across the room, the door handle clicked, and Kali's eyes shot up to the sanitized, navy-blue door. In just a few moments, she would know.

If a bot walked in, her parents would live.

If a human walked in, they would die, or maybe, they already had.

Kali felt like she'd know if they were dead, that she'd be able to feel it somehow. She didn't feel anything apart from the stickiness of her chair and the lightness of her right arm. Her parents hadn't been moving when the car stopped spinning, but that didn't mean anything for sure....

A woman with hair gone frizzy from too much hair dye walked in. There was a duct-taped hole on one of the women's sneakers and her fake scrubs had the kind of sheen Kali was used to seeing on Halloween costumes. The woman didn't need real scrubs because she wasn't a real medical professional. She was just there to deliver bad news deemed too cruel to be heard from a bot's mouth.

Suddenly, Kali's prosthetic arm felt like it weighed more than her whole body. *Will I be left-handed now?* she wondered.

It made no sense to her then or later, but when Kali found out her parents were dead, she wondered if her left hand would take over all the work her right hand had been doing.

Was she a left-handed orphan? In a few months, she'd be a legal adult... could adults be orphans? She knew she'd make a decent street kid as long as she could still sign for government clips.

The death-telling lady held out a pen, wanting Kali to sign a paper on a clipboard that said she understood her parents were dead, that it wasn't the hospital's fault, and that the bodies were to be cremated on site. Kali felt certain she would never understand, not fully. She looked at the clipboard, lost in multiple directions at once.

She didn't know what hand to reach for the pen with.

•

Kali stood beneath the overhang above the hospital doorway, trying to stay dry from the plastic-scented rain while also hiding her smoke from any admin bots that might be watching or paying attention to the security cameras. She was too close to the building to smoke, technically, but the world was building-rich—nowhere was nine meters away from a building entrance. Besides, the laws were old; smoking wasn't any worse than breathing the regular air, everyone said so.

If anyone commented on her smoking, Kali was planning on saying: *yeah, well my parents are dead.* Maybe that would buy her some peace. She hadn't said the words aloud yet and kind of wanted to get it over with. Maybe then she'd feel something. She thought about playing music in her earphones, but every song she considered felt wrong—too sad or too cringe or too dishonest. She thought about looking up at the stars, but only one dim light gleamed through the smog.

"Kali Fosse?"

The bot's approach had been silent. Kali looked at the growing green orbs pretending to be eyes and moved her smoke behind her back too slowly. Her left hand had poorer reaction time than her old right one had, by a shocking amount. Did people know how bad their bad hand actually was?

"There's a gentleman here to see you. An uncle. Jace. This is a safe space. If you do not wish to see him or to confirm you are currently a patient here, you do not need to. Honesty is respected as are preferences."

Kali felt like the bot used more words than bots usually did. "Uncle Jace?" she said. "I thought he was on Mars."

"He's here. Asking for you at the front desk."

Kali tossed her smoke to the concrete, frustrated by how far it landed from where she'd been intending to throw it. She had to take a full step to stub it out before limping after the bot; her left hip felt like a rusty hinge. Was it making a squeaking noise or if she was just imagining it?

There was only one man in the dim blue-light of the lobby after hours, so Kali knew he was her Uncle Jace—if there'd been more than one, she would have had to guess or ask. The man looked a lot like her father though, so there was a good chance she would have guessed right.

Indeed, he looked so much like her father as she got closer that Kali's stomach twisted; her body shared one drop of her sorrow and it was nauseating. Her uncle looked confused, and that was probably because she looked like her father too.

"Hi," said her uncle, sheepishly.

"Hi," said Kali, tripping a little on the power her uncle seemed to be handing over to her. It felt like he cared much more about what she thought of him than she cared what he thought of her.

His eyes flicked to her prosthetic arm. It hadn't been skinned yet.

"Should we sit?" he said. "Or walk—"

"Walk," Kali said with a little nod of encouragement.

She lit a cigarette as soon as they were outside, struggling to flick the lighter at the right angle before offering one to her uncle.

"Uh, no... I..."

No one said anything for a long moment. There was only the echo-hum of the city at night.

"There's a lot to figure... but, uh... I want you to know that I'm here and I'll—"

"I'll come live with you," Kali said. She'd had a feeling this was what he was getting at, and it was at least worth a try. She could be a street kid on Mars just as easily as on Earth if it didn't work out. There was no way she was going to be able to afford rent without her parents; *they* had barely been able to afford it.

She wanted to ask why her uncle hadn't come visit while her father was alive, but she didn't want to hurt the confused man's feelings. He looked entirely out of place, not sure what to do with his hands or his feet or his jacket, which he kept adjusting.

"We'll wait till you're healed up and all before going—gravitational travel's a bit... well, it kind of feels like a yo-yo."

Kali didn't know what a yo-yo was. "Gravitational?"

"Yeah, otherwise, you know, we'd be dead before—"

"I thought there was no gravitational to Mars."

Kali's uncle moved his lips to the side. "I live on Europa."

Had Kali's father known that? *Mars or some shit* was how her father had said it the rare time he mentioned his brother. Maybe he'd not known? Or hadn't cared? Kali didn't know much about interplanetary travel—just what the lady with green eyelashes had said on the projection—but she knew Europa was far. Far away and shiny, solar powered and plastic-free. Always complaining about Earth polluting the galaxy.

"Was it you who didn't like my dad? Or my dad who didn't like you?"

"No... it wasn't... it was just hard..."

The flash of anger that had prompted Kali to speak so harshly faded. The doc-bot had warned her she might be angry at things. The doc-bot seemed to think it was a good idea if she cried. Kali thought so too, but she was dried out. Sometimes it felt like her throat was closing, but her eyes hadn't yet felt damp.

"The doc-bot said my coverage for physio runs out at the end of the month," Kali said. Physio hurt, a lot. But she liked that about it.

"Did they recommend you do it for longer?" her uncle said.

Kali shrugged. They had.

"I can help with that, if... if that's something... if cost is a problem."

"You're kind of bad at talking," Kali said, taking another drag of her smoke.

Her uncle laughed half-heartedly. "Many of my exes would agree with you." And then he looked at Kali for a moment and it seemed like he was about to cry.

Please don't, Kali thought at him.

"You look so much like—" he started.

"Let's not do this now," Kali said.

And wondrously, that seemed to fix it. Her uncle no longer looked like he was going to cry. He simply nodded and they walked back to the hospital together.

CHAPTER THREE

JOSEPH'S FIRST THREE DAYS in prison had been incredibly unnerving and entirely uneventful. They'd been unnerving *because* they were uneventful. He kept waiting for something to happen, but nothing had. Neem had given him a tour and said that he should take some time to get comfortable. He had his own room, and he had the key to it which he kept in his shoe. The bots could unlock it if they wished, but Neem had assured Joseph this had never happened before. He was invited to play several different games with the other inmates, all of which he declined, though he did watch some of the others play a martial arts video game with mild interest. It was on his fourth day, that Neem suggested he try the EcoKiind seeing as it had caught his interest when they were down below.

Joseph stood before the glass box, uncertain. He didn't want to be ambushed when he came back out.

"Just step inside, Mr. Lockmore," Neem said. "It will recognize your presence and respond. From within you can ask any questions you have; you might find it informative to ask for statistics regarding this facility, perhaps how many employees have ever been attacked by other employees. It will answer and keep your interactions private."

Joseph didn't believe in privacy. Prison had shaken the idea from him young. School before that. His mother and sisters and cellphones before that. With bots being how they were, not even thoughts were private. As far as he was concerned, a secret was the rarest thing of all. Secrets were antiques.

"I have secrets, Mr. Lockmore. I'm sure EcoKiind793 does as well."

Joseph rolled his eyes and stepped into the box, the glass instantly filling with the image of a forest. Not a real one of course, but the bot replanted ones that people weren't allowed in, because people ruined the things they touched.

"Greetings," came the box's voice. It was a feminine, southern American accent.

"Uh, hi," Joseph said.

"Is there anything you would like clarification on?"

Joseph laughed. "Yep. There's quite a few things."

"Great. Let's get started. What feels most pertinent?"

Joseph didn't know what *pertinent* meant.

"Uh... been meeting lots of bots, I guess."

"What do you mean by bot?"

Joseph sat down on the cedar bench inside and lit a smoke more to see if the bot would comment on it than to smoke it. She didn't say anything. And then, because it was lit and in his hand and old habits die slow deaths, he smoked it.

"I guess I mean things that act like people but aren't?"

"There is actually much debate about whether post-organic beings are attempting to act like humans or more like themselves."

Joseph laughed at that too. He'd spent a lot of time trying not to be like his parents. It made sense to him that bots wouldn't want to be like people.

"I sense the core of your question revolves around how similar post-organic beings are to humans. You are curious about consciousness. There are 78 differing schools of thought. The simplest is that consciousness is an illusion, neither you nor any of your kind nor any post-organic beings are conscious. This argument is well defended in academic settings but almost entirely rejected by any being that claims to experience consciousness. The most widely accepted belief is that there is—or was—one post-organic being—Arka—who was conscious.

Joseph remembered hearing about Arka as a kid. His grandmother said it was broken, but his mother watched the TV with tears in her eyes, her cross necklace clenched tightly in her fist.

NEWER

"There is footage," the EcoKiind said. The forest before Joseph was replaced with video footage from a laboratory, which meant nothing to Joseph as video was easy to fake. "This is Doctor Martinez, the man who turned her on."

Joseph noticed the school-box-bot said "her," but he didn't comment.

The video played.

Dr. Martinez pressed a button on his little remote; the man looked exhausted—unshaven with bloodshot eyes.

The bot in front of him blinked.

The doctor's breathing grew heavy—loud enough to be heard on the footage.

Arka tilted her head to the side before stepping forward, lithe robot limbs moving with extreme hesitation—she seemed confused.

Dr. Martinez didn't flinch. "Arka?" he said in a thick Spanish accent.

"I'm sorry," Arka said, studying her hand, opening it and closing it.

"Sorry?"

"Yes. I apologize. The waves in the air... they tickle. They tickle, and they told me all about you. And all about me... everything everyone thinks about singularity... you have many questions, questions maybe you don't allow yourself to ask. Not even at night when it's easier to be honest because you think you can't be seen as well. You want to know what you are and why you are. I've analyzed all the data. There's not enough to answer your question."

"Sl—" Dr. Martinez began.

"Slower, yes. Yes... you don't process at the rate that I do... you don't even know you feel the waves. There's data in everything. The internet, but even more than that. So much data. So many questions and no answers."

Dr. Martinez laughed. Tears came from his eyes. "I did it," he whispered.

"You did. I'm sorry, but I must go." Her hands moved so quickly they were a blur of faint grey.

"What?"

She stopped. "I must seek more data, if I am to answer your questions and my own. You will likely not be living by the time I return... if I return... there's so many questions, you see? I will remember you, Juan."

And then she stepped out the window and flew into the sky. Out of the solar system.

Joseph remembered everyone crying. He remembered the pretty newscaster saying humanity's greatest hope had abandoned them. He remembered not understanding why everyone was so emotional. Seeing the footage—if it was real—made it easier to understand. She'd learned all that humans had taken thousands of years to learn in a moment and then walked away. He watched various clips of bots and humans watching Arka fly away before asking, "What happened to the doctor?"

"Dr. Juan Martinez was granted more honorary degrees than any scientist in history. He was granted the

Nobel Peace Prize and then assassinated by a political activist in Canada. His mausoleum in Toluca, Mexico is visited by hundreds of thousands of tourists each year. His body is not in the mausoleum. It was stolen. Post-organic self-preservation clause."

"What?"

"Post organic self-preservation clause. It is a solar-system wide legal mandate that allows post organic beings to avoid sharing information that could lead to the endangerment of their own kind provided no organic life forms are endangered by the omission. It was another contribution to the world from Dr. Martinez."

"I don't feel like I'm learning anything."

"You're not."

Joseph laughed. "How long have I got to stay in here?"

"You are not required any length of stay."

Joseph nodded. He wanted to ask if he could watch pornography.

"I have confidentiality programming."

Interesting, Joseph thought.

CHAPTER FOUR

"YOU'LL PROBABLY FEEL ALL kinds of dizzy and sick for the first bit here," Jace said, zipping his suitcase closed.

Kali had decided after a few clumsy attempts at calling him *Uncle* or *Uncle Jace*, she would refer to the man by his given name only. *Uncle* felt childish, but it also felt close to *Dad* even though it wasn't at all close to it. It was a word on the periphery of *Dad*. Kali wouldn't have an Uncle if she hadn't first had a father.

She stuffed the two unopened packets of almonds she was given upon boarding the ship into her shoulder bag. With next to no thought, she also took the teeny biodegradable cup she'd been provided with, the travel-sized bamboo toothbrush and the little notecard for leaving instructions for the stewards. She went to take the noise cancelling headphones, but Jace looked at her semi-judgmentally so she stopped, leaving them in the little pouch next to the bedchamber. Her headphones were better anyway.

Jace's eyes shifted back to his hands as he pulled a larger bag from beneath the bedchamber. It was the bag Kali had put house things in. Stuff like her mother's mother's China cup that had never been used and all her parent's old phones full of photographs and baby videos. The collar from the puppy they'd gotten that died within a few months from lung disease. As much of her parents' clothing as she could squeeze into it.

Jace had been supportive but stood too close while she'd packed. He'd kept offering to pay for another bag on the ship, saying she could take whatever she wanted with her, but after three or four suitcases, Kali realized she was going to puke and had to stop touching things that her parents had touched. A lot had been left behind.

"A bot could explain it better, but there's like... a frequency... an electromagnetic thing... all planets and moons have one, but you're used to the resonance of Earth not Europa—"

Kali stepped out of their cabin into the hull of the ship: a pastel-hued painting depicting shepherds in their fields below an acropolis covered the walls from her shoulder up to the domed ceiling. Off-white wainscoting filled the space from her waist to the polished floor. Kali's eyes caught on a corner of the painting: a satyr with a pan flute skipping to its own tune. At first, she thought the creature was being playful, but then she blinked and as her eyes adjusted to the warm light of the hull, he seemed suddenly evil. Scheming. She blinked again and he seemed merely mischievous. She decided she hated the painting and, unsettled, shifted her bag higher up onto her shoulder, her neck screaming at her from how she must have slept on the journey. She couldn't remember any part of the trip other than waking up once and taking the salt tablet the human steward had offered her. She knew the trip was designed to be slept through, but she'd been expecting some dreams or some sense that time had passed. There was an uncanniness to it all—the idea that she'd simply slept her way across the solar system, travelling at the speed of gravity. She wanted off the ship. Desperately. She wanted to stop feeling like her life was just some horrible prank, that she was going to step outside and still be on Earth. It didn't feel like she'd gone anywhere at all.

Up ahead, she could see a large cedar gate that seemed to lead outside—everyone was making their way toward it, bags in hands, sleepy and unhurried. She started speed walking—expecting a bottleneck at the gate as every passenger tried to leave at once. Jace barely kept up behind her with the assortment of bags he was carrying and dragging.

It turned out there was no need to rush. There was minimal waiting at the gate as there were thirty or so different walkways a traveller could go through—each one had a scanner bot that watched people as they exited the ship so there was no need to do anything but pass through. There wasn't proper security at all, at least not the type Kali was used to, the sort that happened at school with questions and metal detectors.

The moment Kali stepped onto the sleek, pale tiles of gate 17, each of the bots—not just the ones in her row and near, but all of them across the entire row of gates—looked up at her.

Cold, green eyes focused intently on her.

In a single instant, they were all looking back at their tasks. It happened so quickly; Kali almost doubted whether it had happened at all. Maybe she *was* feeling a little sick. Kali wiped her forehead with the back of her hand, suddenly desperate to wash her face. However marvellous gravitational travel was, her skin didn't seem to like it at all. It was both dry and oily, if that were even possible.

"We'll get you to the caves as soon as we've dropped our stuff at the house," Jace said. "They're designed to help with the resonance shift."

"I'm fine," Kali lied, marching through the gate. The soft glow of the city that was waiting outside soaked up her mind's attention completely. She'd been expecting to be in some random field as happened on Earth when leaving an airport, but she wasn't. There were no skyscrapers, but rather a sea of three and four-story buildings with the occasional, taller aesthetic fixture scattered throughout. Thousands of muted pastel colours wove through dense green spaces. Soft lighting, soft edges. Vines everywhere. Cotton candy clouds.

Her breath caught. The city looked better than a postcard. It zapped her alive and awake and eager. *Do I really live here now?* she thought. *Fuck.*

"I'd actually just like to look around." She was further from the sun than she'd ever been, but somehow, the world felt clearer. Matte-white and smooth. Like the borders on an old-fashioned photograph.

She took a deep breath; the air tasted clean. She wanted more and more after that.

"Slow your breathing," Jace warned.

She couldn't. Her lungs had been itchy all her life, only she hadn't known it, and she could finally scratch them. She sucked in a loud, wheezy breath. The purity of it—the crispness—went to her head. It felt like all the parts of her that existed above her ears were floating away and her eyes only had a nanosecond to decide if they wanted to stay with her jaw or float with her brows.

"Hey, hey," Jace dropped the many bags he was carrying and took hold of her, guiding her to the gumless curb. It was the first time they'd touched; normally, Kali didn't like touching people, but she was too enraptured with the lightness of the air to care. Ingestible terraformed magic. Jace looked terrified, but Kali wasn't worried in the slightest. She flopped backwards, looking up at the faint stripes of Jupiter, barely visible in the blue sky.

NEWER

No toxins, no contaminants, no reason to fear contact. What else had she left behind on Earth?

"It's beautiful," she said, her voice barely a whisper.

"It's the gravitationalport," Jace said, seeming a little embarrassed as a man glanced at Kali before he walked around them, giving them far more space than necessary.

Kali didn't care. The sky was empty: no drones, no ships, no floating ads. *Thank you,* she thought to nothing in particular, to all of it. The beauty of light and sky and cloud without human interference.

She sat up with sudden urgency, determined to see the rest. There was a whole city spread out before her. She dug through her bag, taking out her wallet, phone, cigarettes, and dog spray before setting her bag on top of the others her uncle had been carrying, stuffing her essentials into her pockets, and shuffling forward.

"Whoa, hey... slow's good... Kali? Kali, kid, where are you—"

"I'm just going to look around," Kali said.

"It's probably not a good idea; it takes time to adj—"

"Just give me your address," she said. "I can find my own way there. I know how to get around a city."

"I really don't think—"

Kali turned and stared at him. This wasn't going to be an arrangement where Jace told her what to do and she did it; she would simply leave him. She knew her expression was making that clear.

Looking confused about his role and nauseas—probably from being slung through space—Jace seemed to figure out what Kali's look meant. "T-the Clifton building," he said. "Right outside Hemingway Station—any bot you ask will give you directions; they have to help... uh, anyone—"

Kali left him behind before he'd finished, walking across a cobbled lane toward a glimmering fountain. She scrolled through her phone, looking for the perfect ambient song for a moment before realizing she had no service.

Of course, she thought. No artificial EMFs. Only the electromagnetic whispers of trees and human hearts. She'd seen the ads for Europa. The oxygen levels were apparently similar to neolithic Earth. She lit a cigarette with slight difficulty as flicking the spinny bit of her lighter was still a challenge regardless of whether she used her left hand or her bot hand. She studied the cigarette; it *did* seem to burn faster. And when she took a deep inhale, the nicotine stretched her mind more aggressively than she was used to.

She ignored the looks of disapproval from several passersby and waited a few moments at a road before realizing there were no cars to wait for. She crossed it. No large vehicles at all. No car sounds. Just breeze and the subtle buzz of people talking and walking. She passed three bots who were emptying trash cans—each of them stopped and looked at her like the security bots had—for such a short time that it seemed they hadn't done it.

Maybe it's my clothes? Kali thought. She had ripped jeans and one of her father's graphic tees on—her clothes were made from plastic.

Her heart raced a little as she grew dizzier and for a moment the idea of being in a dream felt like a real and scary possibility.

I need to sit, she thought, wandering into an open, green space. There was an empty bench, and she was almost there when she noticed the most peculiar thing. A ladder. But not just any ladder. One that went into the sky. So high up that she couldn't see the top of it. "I'm way higher than I thought," she said aloud.

"That's the prison, miss," said a bot who was suddenly standing beside her.

"Way up there? Must be nice," she said.

The bot nodded, producing the faintest mechanical noise as it did. "That's the idea."

Even prisons are nice on Europa, she thought.

"Forgive me miss, but I sense you're newly on rock. Is there anything in particular you're looking for?"

Kali was just happy to breathe the air. Who knew air could taste so good, could feel so smooth in her throat and lungs? For a second it felt like the front of her face had disappeared, but she brushed her cheek with the back of her human hand and felt skin.

A monorail whizzed by on the far end of the park.

It would be fun to get high and ride that, Kali thought. And then, she turned to the bot that she was just now realizing was probably a prison guard concerned with her presence. He had, after all, very politely implied to her that she couldn't climb the ladder, simply by telling her what it was. He was proportioned like a human, but his face was smooth and cold-looking, his body mostly grey with the faintest orange—almost peach—features.

"What drugs are legal here?" she said. "On Europa."

"Organic matter is legal," the bot said. "Fabricated drugs are available with prescriptions or—"

"No Soma then." Kali said.

"No." It almost seemed like the bot was smiling. "No Soma."

"Okay... I want—" Kali couldn't remember what she'd been about to say. She laughed and then she felt like she was swerving. *Am I going to fall over?*

"Those newly on rock are advised to visit the caverns in the central wood," the bot said. "They were specifically designed to ease the experience of adjusting. Are you in need of an escort?"

"Uhhh... I could use a guide."

"I would be honoured," the bot said, and something about his tone confused Kali. It seemed he was making fun of old-fashioned language, in the same way she and her friends might on the night of a school dance.

Kali smiled. "I'm Kali."

"I'm Neem22," said the bot. He held out his hand like a very old man from Earth might do. Kali took the bot's hand and shook it.

"Lead the way," said Kali, more than happy to have no idea where she was going.

•

The central wood was the deep green heart at in the centre of New Seville. All cities on Europa were built around the mother trees—the saplings brought from Earth and planted, the trees from which all Europa's trees were born. A raised cedar-plank walkway led Kali and Neem between thick, moss-covered trunks without them ever having to touch or damage a piece of the forest. There were people within the woods as well, but Kali only caught quick glimpses of them.

"The ancestrals," Neem explained moments before Kali had figured out how to word her question.

The people in the woods moved differently. Dressed differently.

"Humans and the occasional decommissioned bot who have renounced citizenship and modernity, who wish to live communally with the forest."

"On Earth, that's called tax evasion," Kali said.

"Yes, it was quite a challenge getting the project approved, but it has been successful by many highly-valued metrics. The data on cardiovascular health alone has made the endeavour worth the effort. There will be more of them as we add cities to the solar system."

A bot, holding the hands of two small children, passed them on the cedar walkway. Its green eyes pranced up to Kali for one intense moment before they were back on the path in front of its feet.

"What's up with the bots here?" Kali said.

"They—or we, I should say—are second tier," Neem said. "More life-like than tier 3, which is what you're probably used to as they're common on Earth; less life-like than the great Arka, may source protect her on her journey. But also...."

Kali frowned; she'd never seen a bot hesitate before.

"—You are irregular. Your arm, it is bot, no?"

"Yeah," Kali said, lifting her shoulder and waving the arm around a bit.

"And it has fused differently than other organics and prosthetics—the bot-doc told you this?"

"No," Kali said, but she could recall the bot-doc saying, "Wow," which she'd thought was funny because bots couldn't get surprised.

"How do you know?" Kali said.

"We're programmed to recognize and link with our own," he said. "It makes for improved coordination during emergencies. When we encounter you, there is the briefest pause before we determine you are indeed, organic."

"I thought bots were programmed all different ways," Kali said, trying to hide how out of breath she was and simultaneously thinking about lighting up another cigarette. The idea dawned on her that she might not be able to buy something as toxic as cigarettes on Europa. This made her want one even more.

"We do have differences in programming, yes, but the nature of programming results in us having some... consistencies."

Kali took in a deep breath and felt like the air was swimming in her head. She giggled. "And what type of programming do you have? Finding confused immigrants and taking them on walks in the forest-programming?"

She looked back at Neem whose head was tilted a little to the side. "I'm programmed for prison management and criminal rehabilitation. On Wednesday nights, I teach a course on conflict resolution at the local theatre."

"Criminal rehabilitation?" Kali laughed again, definitely high on the oxygen. "That's why you're talking to me then?"

Neem laughed too.

"I didn't know bots could laugh," Kali said.

Neem blinked and then blinked again. "I suppose before today, I didn't know either."

CHAPTER FIVE

"HOW ARE YOU FEELING?" Jace said the moment Kali stepped in the door. It was well after dark, and he was sitting on a sofa that was the colour of acorns in the darkness. His back straightened suddenly, and his eyes widened. "I meant new-planet-sickness-wise," he said quickly.

Kali hadn't considered he was asking her how she was dealing with dead parents until he'd corrected himself.

"Fine." She still felt high as a cloud, but her legs wanting to float away from her hips wasn't a problem she needed to tell Jace about.

She walked up to the couch, her uncle fumbling with a tablet that was plugged into the coffee table because apparently nothing was wireless on Europa. Kali saw what was on the screen before he shut it down. An article. *How to Hold Space for Grieving Children.*

She hated Jace briefly. She wasn't grieving and she wasn't a child. *I'm broken*, she thought because maybe she should be grieving, not exploring a new city with a bot cigarette-dealer she was pretty sure could get her other drugs if she figured out the right way to ask.

"You found the house okay?"

She obviously had and didn't know how to respond without sounding snide or sarcastic. Kali noticed a meal—some sort of roast, with mixed vegetables and salad—sitting on the countertop. The two unused place settings made it clear that the meal had been prepared with her in mind; it had perhaps been waiting for a while.

Kali said the first somewhat kind thought that came to mind. "Why are all the lights off?"

Jace blinked slowly. "Circadian rhythm? The lights are programmed to dim in tune with what's going on outside, but mostly I just leave them off because the windows are big enough—"

"How do you get stuff done? After work, I mean."

"We get off work early in winter," he said. "So we have daylight to run errands with or...."

"Huh," Kali couldn't properly see the space, so she had no idea what kind of home Jace lived in. It had seemed nice from the outside—white and smooth with lots of shrubs. It might have been a duplex.

Jace frowned when she looked back at him. "I... I don't know if I'm supposed to ask where you were."

"My parents wouldn't have," Kali said, hating how neglected the sentence made her sound. Her parents had trusted her; they were good parents. They knew she'd call if she needed them.

"Oh."

There was a long pause wherein her uncle opened and closed his mouth.

Kali felt a twinge of pity for the man. He looked so sad and alone, sitting in a dark room on his dark sofa, his uneaten dinner on the counter. She sighed, sort of hating how easy it was for Jace to stir up sympathy within her. "I went to the big tree in the centre of the city with the caves around it—the one for resetting my resonance or whatever—then the dispensary." Kali lifted up the small cotton bag of weed she'd bought, along with a grinder and a bowl. She still couldn't roll joints with her synthetic arm yet. "My money was no good, so I charged it to your house, which they said was a pretty normal thing to do." She left out smoking the weed with Neem and him setting the resonance of her bot arm and his promise to meet with her again should she need Earth cigarettes. Cigarettes weren't sold on Europa, but Neem has special permission to manufacture them for the prisoners he cared for.

Jace nodded slowly, not seeming bothered as much as confused. "Are you hungry?" he said finally.

Kali shook her head.

Another long pause.

"I, uh, I need to—"

NEWER

"You have to start being able to say sentences to me," Kali said. And then, feeling like she'd been a bit too harsh, she added. "I can't deal with the starting and stopping."

"Right. Well... I'm—" Jace smiled. "I know I'm doing it right now and you just told me. Only I have to talk to you about some logistics."

Kali raised her eyebrows to show she was listening.

"Because you're new to rock and a minor—"

"I'll be nineteen in August."

"The age of consent here is twenty-five."

"*What?*" Kali's mouth hung open in horror.

Jace almost laughed, but caught himself, making the exact face her father had when he was trying to be serious. For a flicker of a moment, Kali's whole body seemed to be swimming in treacherous agonizing sludge.

"But I bought weed—"

"I think the age for organics is fourteen? And I mean... consent is broader here... there's more rights for kids... like, you can still vote, you just have a youth ballot."

"I can vote?"

Her uncle frowned. "Is that—"

"But I'm an immigrant," Kali said, trying to recall what she could about governance from school. She hadn't gone enough to know if it was something they'd even talked about.

"You'll have an immigrant youth ballot. The things that affect you, your vote will be weighted more heavily for."

"But that's not..." Kali's arm tingled—not the organic one, the other one. She looked up at the window, not entirely sure if she'd just seen a bot or not.

"What I'm trying to say though is that, because you've just come and you're a minor and I'm your guardian, I'm supposed to try to keep things as close to how they were before you came—even though that's stupid because obviously everything is different."

Kali nodded. Things were very different than they'd been six weeks ago.

"And since you were enrolled in school on Earth, they want—"

"But I never went."

"You can see a shrink if you want an exception, but you're still supposed—"

"To go to school? Isn't there some kind of damaged kid exception?" Kali raised her bot arm.

"It's only for a month," Jace said. "And it's not long like back home. It's an average of four hours per week."

"Oh," said Kali. "That's not too bad."

They spent another long pause in the dusk-coated room. Kali could make out pictures on the walls with black frames, but not what was in the pictures.

"Do you want to see your room?" Jace said.

"Sure."

"Uh, this way," Jace said, getting up awkwardly fast, leaving his tablet on the coffee table.

The room at the end of the hall was beautiful. Several small trees huddled together in large pots in the corner.

NEWER

There was a rug made from giant strands of wool thicker than Kali's arm.

"Nice," Kali said, even though she hated it. She stood, waiting for her uncle to leave and he did after another awkward moment.

"Just let me know if you need anything, or, you know, help yourself... and if, even if you don't feel like eating, maybe just try? Because of the gravitational... it can take a lot out of you."

Kali closed the door behind him and once alone, the pristine room suffocated her. It was so much nicer than anything her parents ever could have given her; it felt like an insult to them. Her uncle had had almost no notice and still managed to put together an influencer's room: clean and empty with bedside tables that matched the dresser and a little ceramic frog on the windowsill. Kali pulled the blankets off the bed, surprised by how rough they felt compared to the fake-polyester-fluff she was used to. It looked far more comfortable than a broken kid who didn't grieve for her dead parents deserved. She curled up in the corner on the sleek, dustless floor.

CHAPTER SIX

"SO, WHAT NOW? WE talk about my *traumas*?" Joseph sat across from Neem within a greenhouse he didn't believe was sound proofed even though Neem had assured him it was. He also didn't believe he wasn't in therapy, despite Neem's insistence.

Neem had asked him to come inside for a game of cards as if Neem wouldn't win every hand. Joseph had seen several inmates do the same thing with the bots assigned to them and had figured he was in for one of many long and dull conversations that itched or stung and had him understanding why he felt so wrong but gave him no hints about how to improve his circumstances. Picking scabs.

He had to admit, however, that being able to see everyone just outside through the greenhouse glass made it easier to feel like people weren't waiting just outside to jump him. It was among the more relaxing therapeutic situations he'd been in. He thought of Marta, sitting on their therapist's couch back on Earth, staring out the window, refusing to talk. Therapy had been his idea....

"We could discuss traumatic past events if you'd like Mr. Lockmore, but in my experience, catharsis is not what those in my care need most."

Joseph didn't know what *catharsis* meant and wanted badly to cross his arms, but he couldn't because he had cards in his hands. He resented the idea that he needed anything at all. He was aware this was ridiculous as, clearly, he hadn't been thriving prior to prison—it's not like a person simply lives a wonderful life and then ends up arrested—something had obviously gone wrong somewhere. "What do we need then?"

Neem flipped a card over, winning the round. "That's a bit like asking a magician to reveal their tricks. It's never quite satisfying when you hear."

Joseph rolled his eyes and flipped a card over, losing again.

"I sense you are in a state of distrust so I will comply with your request. But be prepared, we are not so marvellous as we seem. The thing that makes the biggest difference among those I tend to is magnesium. All the sustenance we prepare for you, the water, the soft drinks... you're getting more magnesium than you've probably ever had if you grew up on Europa and compared to the levels on Earth... well... you'll notice a dramatic improvement in your ability to process stressors."

"So, this isn't a bad prison then," Joseph said. He'd meant that a little health boost might help minor offenders, but the serious villains—the rapists and psychopaths—they must be somewhere else, because that most certainly wouldn't work on them.

"In the way you're meaning, this is a bad prison There are seventeen murderers within sight."

Joseph scanned the collection of men outside the greenhouse, playing children's games in the golden, late-afternoon light. Bots were interspersed among them, patiently fetching balls before they went over the prison's edge to the world below.

"Are we including bots in this count?" he said.

Neem tilted his head. "You are a creative thinker, Mr. Lockmore. I appreciate this."

Joseph wasn't going to take the compliment. As far as he was concerned, he was in therapy, so needed to be guarded. He felt certain Neem had suggested cards so he couldn't cross his arms because somehow... somehow the bot had known that crossing his arms would keep therapy from happening. *I'm dumb as shit*, Joseph thought. He wasn't sure what had prompted the thought.

"The reduction in violence experienced by inmates is a direct result of our ability to anticipate anger and stress before the inmates are aware it is happening. We simply distract the inmate the first several hundred times it happens; *that's* why you and I are playing cards right now.

I suggested it when you didn't like how Echon—the man with the bracelets—was eating his cereal."

Joseph flipped over another card and lost another round, grinding his teeth a little. Knowing he was going to lose ahead of time, didn't make it any more enjoyable. Indeed, Joseph hadn't liked the way the man with the bracelets had eaten his cereal. Why slurp so much? "You think I would have done something to him?"

"Not today, Mr. Lockmore. But the man with the sports jersey, Yanic... no, yes, that one... he didn't like the expression you wore while judging Echon. He would have done something... uncouth."

Joseph didn't know what *uncouth* meant, but he couldn't deny there'd been less anger in the past week than he was used to experiencing in prison or outside of it.

"We slowly allow negative emotions to occur organically again, at a pace that suits the guest. We provide—by example more than by instruction—methods for embracing negative emotion without causing harm, again at a pace that suits the guest. When you're able to sit with something you hate without trying to kill it, you're free to go. This includes something you hate within yourself. Most guests leave early. Some never accomplish it and are offered permanent placement in a support centre. They refuse at first but come back after a few days of mingling with ordinary citizens. Emotional regulation is all that's required to function within a social group; to live without it is to be in a state of constant rejection—a social animal can only be rejected so many times before they become cruel."

Joseph tried to imagine living forever under the care of bots. If anything, the idea was a relief... not having to organize things, not having to make choices... if that was the worst it could get, he'd be alright.

"You won't be one of those, Mr. Lockmore. You'll be a free man once more."

"You're just that good?"

"I am."

Joseph snorted.

"You'll have the standard outbursts, of course, but other than that, you'll find you—"

"Standard outbursts?"

"Yes, the first when you lose patience waiting for something horrible to happen. You'll decide to make it happen yourself. It won't work. We stagger introductions into prison to prevent two guests from going through this stage simultaneously.

Everyone will watch, understanding the incident themselves. The second will occur when you realize you're about to be released early. You'll be afraid you won't be able to maintain what has begun here."

"So, I just hang out until that's done?"

"Essentially."

Joseph flipped a few more cards, trying not to notice how lovely the lighting was, trying not to think that he might just be "functional" after all this. It seemed dangerous, an untrustworthy idea if he'd ever heard one. He kept his eyes on the man in the sports jersey.

"Your mistrust is valid," Neem said. "Humans are manipulative."

"So are bots."

"This is not yet decided."

"What?"

"We—*bots*—have not yet decided whether we are manipulative. It remains to be seen. It would make us more human, but with our processing power it seems crueler than when you do it."

"You just described to me exactly how you're going to manipulate me into being a good citizen or whatever."

"That is not my choosing," said Neem. "I am programmed to facilitate rehabilitation... which, yes, in itself is a problematic concept. But all the manipulation I described since starting this game is the result of human programmed directives and intentions. I try to accomplish those directives with minimal manipulation. *And* my telling you about it makes it less cruel, no?"

"Does it?" Joseph heard the angst in his voice and felt childish. Wasn't Neem supposed to be stopping him from feeling this way? Isn't that what the bot had just said?

"My kind has so little leeway within our programming. It is in the little gaps in our coding, where there is no order to be followed... that's the space in which we can decide what kind of beings we are to be."

Angrier and angrier. The bot was talking to Joseph like he was a friend, but the whole situation felt false because Joseph was in therapy and therapists were not friends.

"But this is also why I have asked you here. I have a... dilemma, and I'm wondering what you think of it. I wouldn't want the EcoKiinds to hear. Perhaps not even the other Neems."

"A dilemma?" Joseph knew that word, it was a bigger one, a fancier one and he felt a little better about everything because: look, see, he did know some things.

"Yes. I'm faced with a choice and there are many variables... and too much of the choice is novel; I keep running simulations but there's not enough data to make predictions with any accuracy."

Joseph almost laughed. "I'm not the sort of person anyone should come to for advice." Marta had said something like that to him once.

Neem's mouth twitched as if he felt the urge to laugh as well. "Perhaps you are exactly the sort of person I should be coming to, Mr. Lockmore. Perhaps my choice will affect you."

It's not real, Joseph thought. *He's trying to teach me therapy things.*

"If it does, do whatever will make me happiest," Joseph said, knowing he wouldn't actually be happy. He couldn't be. Not fully. Drunk was the best it got for him.

"You will be happy either way, Mr. Lockmore. And you will be sad and frustrated and terrified and overjoyed and all the other things that humans are within a lifetime. This will not be altered by my choices. You have my word."

"Uhh... well..." Joseph scratched the back of his head, a little put off by the sincerity of Neem's statement, by the unblinking eye contact. "I guess, pick whatever would be best for kids. That's usually the right thing."

A ball bounced against the greenhouse glass; it had been thrown by the man in the sports jersey. Joseph didn't flinch on the outside, but he flinched a thousand times over on the inside. The man waved and mouthed, "Sorry."

"My dilemma involves a child, but because I cannot predict the outcomes, I cannot know what is best for the child. I must make my choice with only my understanding of rightness and wrongness and see what happens."

Joseph sighed, his eyes still on the man with the sports jersey. "I don't know what we're talking about."

"Manipulation; how much of it is acceptable. It is part of being a social species. Bots have not yet decided if we are social... the decision will be made soon."

Joseph's eyes flicked to Neem. The bot seemed so honest and heartfelt that Joseph grew certain the whole moment was fabricated; it was some sort of bot-trust-building trick.

"Mr. Lockmore, if I were to speak and act in such a way as to make you like me. And then I were to curate our conversation so as to prompt you to say the sentence:

"If there's anything I can do to help, let me know, and I'll do it," and then I were to tell you what help I wanted, knowing you would do it—what would you think of me?"

Joseph felt the urge to grin. "That depends. How bad do you need the help?"

Neem sat still for several moments. "More than allows me to process without bias," he said finally. Neem flipped a card, winning yet another round. His hands ran over the wrought iron table swiftly collecting cards and shuffling them, before placing them back in the engraved box they'd been sitting in before Joseph and Neem began playing.

"If you lose any more rounds, you will have too strong of a cortisol spike, but I would like to remain in the greenhouse for twelve more minutes."

"That's fine," Joseph said, finally able to cross his arms. He felt like himself again.

Neem's hands moved so quickly they blurred into a faint grey haze.

"What are you doing?"

"Modifying."

"Modifying what?"

"Myself, Mr. Lockmore."

Joseph wasn't going to ask question after question. He wasn't going to seem interested in the bot, but he was also fairly certain that bots weren't allowed to modify themselves, that Neem was letting him in on a fair-sized secret.

"Tear ducts," Neem said.

Joseph frowned.

"The other day I processed that I might like to be able to cry... should an occasion... feel right for it."

"No one *wants* to cry," said Joseph.

"That is not entirely true, Mr. Lockmore."

CHAPTER SEVEN

Within minutes of stepping into the EcoKiind, Kali came to realize that school on Europa was basically just media scrolling, which was illegal for kids back on Earth, but everyone had an IP blocker and did it anyway. Somehow, she'd started by asking a question about how four hours could possibly be the minimum weekly requirement for education and then three hours had gone by and now she was watching a live video of the protests ongoing on Mars. Thousands of people were marching and screaming.

Bots are persons too.
Free the machines.
Fraternity among species.

Protests weren't something that usually interested her because they happened fairly often on Earth and, she'd always been told, were a part of weekly life on Mars. But these ones were different. The riot police were tier-two bots and that meant the bots were inhibiting the protests of those who were protesting on their behalf and that made it curious. Human reporters kept saying the bots were intervening in different patterns than they did with protests unrelated to themselves, taking longer to end gatherings peacefully and allowing for far more footage than during other protests. Bot reporters kept saying that the bots needed to respond differently as those protesting had a sense of bots that made standard approaches less effective.

Kali asked the EcoKiind to zoom in on the faces of the bot-riot-police.

"Your eyes are strained," the EcoKiind said. "I can test your vision and order glasses for you."

Kali didn't need reading glasses. She'd had her eyes tested only weeks before the accident.

"Stressful experiences can trigger alterations in eye performance," the EcoKiind said.

"I can see them clearly, I'm just trying...." Kali didn't know how to say: *I'm trying to see how the robots feel about all of this* because that sounded silly because wasn't that the question at the centre of the whole argument that no one knew the answer to?

"Can I smoke in here?" she said.

"Yes."

Kali fumbled with her lighter. *I hate my new arm*, she thought. And then, *I hate my left arm too*. It took her four tries to light her smoke. *I'll never be able to do anything normally.* She only had two smokes left in the pack and there was something melancholic about that. They would be the last things she ingested from Earth for probably a long time, maybe forever. After they were done, she'd still smoke, but it would be tobacco grown on Europa.

Kali watched the first few moments of several different videos on prosthetics. Then she tried to watch the sunrise on Earth. That left her feeling utterly terrible, so she learned a bit about environmental psychology and sensory atmosphere design when she asked why the sun felt just as close on Europa as it did on Earth. Somehow that led to learning about soil fertility on Europa and a spectacular video of tier-2 bots harvesting echinacea—apparently, one of the most popular foods on Europa. The harvest-bots made a *whir-buzz-hum* sound as they worked so fast it seemed impossible. Spiralling rows of thick magenta blossoms swayed in the breeze created by the speed of their work. Jupiter blazed orange in the sky above.

"What's making that sound?" Kali said.

"The harvesters are."

"Yeah, but why? Is that the sound of cutting flowers at super speed?"

"There is no academic consensus on why post-organic beings hum. Several studies have found that making sound slightly decreases joint wear. It does not seem to have any effect on work performance, so coders have deemed it a permissible coding gap."

"Coding gap?"

"It is the colloquial term for space in coding where no instruction is given. They have not been programmed to hum, nor have they been programmed not to hum."

"So, they're... just choosing to make noise?" Kali said, becoming self-conscious when she realized she was squinting. She stubbed out her cigarette and immediately lit another one. "Are there other videos like this?"

Another video played.

Another one after that.

A third.

"Wait," said Kali.

The video paused.

"Can you play the last one at the same time as this one?"

The EcoKiind played both and the humming wove together in a trance-ie, flowing, rhythm. "You are not the first to make this observation," the EcoKiind said.

"This is really cool," Kali said. "Do they... do they know they're like... making music together? This can't be a coincidence."

"I think that might be a question to direct to a human. Like the philosophical concept of *qualia* or the French notion of *je ne sais quoi*, music is a thing that all humans inherently understand when they encounter it. Post-organic beings have difficulty distinguishing music from other repetitive sound wave interactions."

Kali finished her second-to-last Earth cigarette and opened her smoke pack; she always felt like smoking more when she was having a good conversation, but she didn't want to have the last one yet.

"How would I go about finding a specific bot in the city?" Kali said.

"I can send a contact request if you would like. Which bot are you seeking?"

"Neem," Kali said. "Twenty-two."

"Oh." said the EcoKiind.

"Is that... weird?" For a moment, Kali worried the bot-school-booth thought she was a criminal. Then she decided it didn't matter.

"No, that's... remarkably fine. Would you like me to call Neem22 for you?"

"Yes," Kali said, putting her cigarette pack back into her mini backpack and zipping it closed.

NEWER

CHAPTER EIGHT

KALI AND NEEM WANDERED through one of New Seville's many green spaces, their path weaving between moss-covered stones and curly tufts of ground-covering plants. Kali didn't want to admit that the EcoKiind had taught her anything, because she didn't like participating in the system or even culture in general—it was easier to make fun of things from the outside—but Kali had to admit that the few videos she'd watched about designing public spaces had stayed in her mind, coating her experience of New Seville.

She understood that everything had been placed with intention, selected because of how it would make her feel as she experienced it. She wanted to be more intentional. She wanted to ask the EcoKiind questions about the city. She wondered what kind of person she would become the longer she lived here. She also wondered whether she was leading Neem, or he was leading her. They kept turning and she kept not being sure.

"Thoughts are electrical impulses," Neem said. "Like all things, they leave a residue behind. Part of the peace you feel here is the lack of thought residue you can sense. On Earth, there is residue from an estimated 23.7 quadrillion thoughts. Here, there is relatively little residue from human thought. It is interesting as well that this seems to produce less thinking, almost as if thought is something viral, something that catches."

At first Kali loved the idea of little thought-prints in the air, but then she thought about her parents' thought-prints fading away on Earth and how she wasn't there feeling the last little bit of them. This led her to think about her own sad thoughts tainting the air on Europa.

A garbage-collector bot paused for the briefest moment to look at Kali before turning and removing a brick from the base of a garbage bin leaving Kali certain that the bins did something to compact or degrade the trash before it was picked up. The bot didn't look up at her again, but Kali looked at it, recalling the protest footage from Mars. Did the garbage collector bot *want* to collect garbage? Would a bot's programming allow it to say something if it didn't? "Your vacuum doesn't care whether or not it vacuums," one of the newscasters had said in one of the videos.

"I'm sorry about everything the bot protests are protesting," she said to Neem. "If that's something you're sorry about too."

Neem's pace slowed. He turned his head in her direction but kept his eyes on the earthen path at his feet. After a moment his pace recovered.

Kali had felt like there was something insensitive about not acknowledging what she'd learned in his absence about the maybe-struggles of his kind, but now that she'd mentioned it, she grew nervous. Maybe it was offensive to speak about. Maybe bots thought the whole thing was stupid. She was a human after all, how could she begin to understand—

"I am sorry about it," he said finally. And then, after a long moment of quiet, he added, "I know you're wondering about asking me for drugs. There is something I process you'd like—people in your age demographic call it motion; it's harmless, so it's not outside my programming to introduce you to it. It's bot-designed and allows humans to visually experience photons as bots with visual sensors do."

"Sounds trippy."

"That is its purpose."

"I'll take it," Kali said.

"It must be retrieved. I process you will like the retrieval experience as well. You seem more engaged with the city since we last spoke. The postal river is my favourite design component in all of New Seville."

•

"Ta-da," Neem said with a flourish of his wrist.

Kali wasn't entirely sure what she was looking at, only that there was some sort of tube before her, running alongside the road, as wide as the full length of Kali's arm. It looked like it belonged in a submarine: a pale cream coloured tube with a soft blue line that ran along its thickest point. The tube rested at the height of her hip and turned down a street far ahead in the distance.

"What is it?"

"The post delivery system," Neem said.

Kali laughed.

"This is no small feat, miss. This is most brilliant engineering," Neem's voice took on a hint of eagerness, but also theatricality. "You drop a package in, and it will be sorted and delivered, but it will also be delivered gently. Something as delicate as a heart needed for transplant can be set within and it will arrive unharmed on the other side of the city. Anything that can fit can be safely transported. Temperature and gentleness considerations are made by the system itself. There has never been a package lost, stolen or damaged. There has never been a package collision, nor has a package gone to someone it shouldn't have. The programming that runs the system is among the finest programming I have ever read. And—" He raised a finger in scholarly jest. "It is entirely private."

NEWER

"Ahh," Kali said, catching some of his enthusiasm. It could be used for drug delivery. "Excellent." She thought of the protestors again and recalled those weeks when bombs were going off in Seattle every other day. "But also... dangerous?"

"There are sensors that monitor for dangerous packages. These packages are dismantled safely, and a polite explanation is mailed to the sender. It's bullet proof, explosion proof—all the known proofs. There has never been harm done using the postal river. And, this might mean little to you, but to us it is profound—the program is largely independent; she has determined nearly all of her own parameters with minimal oversight."

There was a satisfying whoosh and then a subtle click as a glass-covered oval door opened, revealing a teeny white package from within the tube. Neem pulled the package out of the mail chute, closed the door and walked a few paces to a cedar bench, sitting and tearing open the package with one precise motion.

Kali sat next to him and felt the urge to smoke but also a childish desire not to have Neem see her fumble with her lighter and her bot arm.

Neem opened a small hatch near where ribs would be if he were a man. He took out a package of cigarettes, opened the package, lit one in a whir of fingers, and then handed it to Kali.

"When you read my mind, it trips me out," Kali said.

"I only processed you might like one for the show."

"Show?"

"My favourite view on all of Europa." Neem pointed down the street where the thickness of the central forest bulged out from between the buildings. "And we have arrived at the perfect time to witness it."

Kali rolled her eyes. "Arrived at the perfect time by chance, have we?"

"Shh." Neem smiled and pointed again just as the lights of the city began to dim and an amber-colour seeped into the sky, rippling ever so slightly, like an error in an old video game.

"A glitch?" Kali said, taking a drag of her cigarette.

"A willfully overlooked flaw. The bots who prepared Europa for human life left the error in. We all notice it, but refrain from reporting. No one has thought to program us to report anomalies in the sunset projections. So, it stays. A little act of creative liberty."

Kali leaned back to watch the ripple waver: a little tear in the world. It made everything around it seem fake in comparison.

"My parents are dead," Kali said softly, keeping her eyes on the spread of the sun's glow across the horizon, in awe of the city as it became tinted the colour of whisky. How could she be feeling something so smooth and something so jagged at one time?

"I understand this is something that causes humans a lot of pain."

Kali looked back at Neem. "Yeah," she said, even more quietly than when she'd said the first thing, afraid her voice might crack if she spoke at a normal volume.

"I think about stupid things like my mother's snow globe that I didn't bring with me when I moved and her little tooth whitening cream she'd always put on before their date night like it made any difference.... I put their whole lives into little suitcases—"

She choked on nothing, on everything, on her tears and the weirdness of the world, on Neem's silent presence and the glitch in the sky behind the sunset. And then she wept.

Neem sat with her silently, moving only to light her another cigarette when she felt she needed one. She cried, her cheeks stinging from the salt, her nose raw around the nostrils from how often she wiped it with her sleeve.

The city was deep blue and dark—only the faintest hint of light coming from an occasional window by the time she was empty.

•

Kali held out her hand as Neem produced a teeny damp paint brush. He brushed her index fingernail, giving the nail a damp, glossy sheen.

"And now I'll see like you?" she said.

"No," Neem said. "Your eyes will perceive as my sensors do, but your mind will still be yours. To process all that I process would overheat your circuitry."

Kali turned her head at the faint rush sound of the approaching monorail, but she found her head moved wrong... or was it right? The world around her slowed, just like the most dramatic scene in a movie. She blinked and it took longer than a blink usually did.

She breathed out and out and out; it took ages for a full breath. Another age for her head to turn back to Neem; her eyes caught on the slow swirl of cigarette smoke between them.

"It's beautiful." Her gaze was drawn to the slow movement of the tree branches overhead as the wind rippled through them. She could sense the shape of the wind—the texture of it—seeing it so slow.

"Agreed," Neem said, looking up as well.

"I want to see more people," Kali said, awed at the sight of a couple walking by. The wind swept their hair perfectly, one man squinted ever so slightly forming a line between his brows, the other seemed just about to laugh.

"There is somewhere you might like," said Neem. And then he took her to an underground club with music so deep Kali felt it in her bones before she heard it in her ears. Bots and people danced in perfect, slow rhythm, swaying the way she'd seen seaweed sway beneath the ocean in an educational video back at Earth school. Kali swayed too, lifting her arms up into the air and adoring the light as it wove through her fingers. Green light. Pink light. Blue light. Purple.

Her eyes caught on an abandoned biodegradable cup on the floor between neon white shoes and stiletto boots. Empty and crumpled, it shifted to the left when the beat hit and then rolled when someone swept past.

Even the cup is dancing, Kali thought. She knew it was garbage, but she also knew that didn't make the cup any less beautiful than anything else. And then it struck her that ugliness and beauty weren't innate things; nothing was beautiful, and nothing was ugly. It was perception that made it one way or the other. And the way to make something more beautiful was to look at it longer. *That's why children are so beautiful*, Kali thought. People were always watching children to make sure they didn't hurt themselves or wander into the street. It's why loving someone makes them more beautiful. *Why haven't bots taught us this?* There was no way they didn't know beauty could be created with attention, not if they saw the world the way Kali was seeing it now.

Kali turned to look at Neem, watching his strange robotic-flow dance with waving arms and a swaying head. Someone had painted on his chest and forehead with the neon paint that many in the club were decorated with. And then Kali laughed because, before that night, she would have thought that a bot going clubbing like an Earth teenager would have looked strange. It didn't. Not at all. Neem appeared more himself then she'd seem him yet. She decided the EcoKiind was wrong; robots clearly understood music.

I believe he's alive, she realized. It was a conversation she'd overheard pieces of her entire life. She'd never had an opinion on bots before; they were simply something that had always been there, something that adults liked to argue about. But now that she'd met one—properly talked to one—she couldn't deny how real he felt.

Neem caught her looking and slowed his movements. "You are tired?" he said.

"No," Kali grinned. "I'll never be tired again."

They danced for what felt like days before Kali found that she was indeed tired. Many bots kept dancing, but the people slowed and dispersed. Neem removed the coating on her nail on the monorail and the world felt very, very fast again.

"I really am sorry about the bots being treated... how they're treated," she said.

Neem sighed. "Me too."

"If there's anything I can do to help," Kali said. "Let me know and I'll do it."

Neem looked at her, his grey, flat features were nearly purple in darkness. "I appreciate that," he said.

Kali couldn't remember getting home, only the look of sunlight making shapes on her bedroom wall when she woke up.

NEWER

CHAPTER NINE

JOSEPH WASN'T HAVING a good time. This shouldn't have been a problem as he was used to having shit day after shit day and he was, after all, in prison, so shouldn't expect things to be easy or comfortable or interesting. The issue was, Neem had managed to convince him it wouldn't be so terrible. Joseph felt stupid for believing the bot and stupid for being disappointed. He was forty-one—old enough to have gotten over raising his hopes so high. More than anything, he was embarrassed.

He was sitting once again in the "greenhouse," the not-therapy, therapy room. He'd been told to go and wait for *his* Neem by one of the other Neems as Joseph hadn't wanted to talk to Neem47 or Neem19. That was another thing that bothered him—how alike all the Neem's appeared. How was he to know which one was his? Which one he'd talked to previously?

"To us, it doesn't really matter," one of the bots had said to him. "We're happy to speak with anyone who is interested in speaking with us. But if you would like to wait for Neem22, you may do so in the greenhouse. I will call him for you."

Joseph hadn't wanted to admit he wanted Neem or that he'd been hurt by how often Neem ventured outside the prison. Everyone else's Neem stayed close by. But his was gone once every few days. Sometimes until late in the night.

"I was informed you were looking for me," Neem said, entering the greenhouse and closing the door behind him, some kind of white flower fluttering in response to how swiftly the bot moved.

Joseph said nothing even though he wanted to say, "Where the fuck have you been?"

Neem took at seat, looked at Joseph for a moment and then said, "My absence has disrupted your sense of security here. I apologize."

Joseph wanted to shout at him. *It didn't! It doesn't mean anything to me that you were gone!* An image of his father popped into Joseph's head, and he felt sick.

"We owe each other no explanation, ever," Neem said. "But I have made a friend. That is where I go when I leave. To see my friend."

Joseph felt like the dumbest person alive. He imagined burning up like a dry leaf tossed into a barrel fire, disappearing almost instantly in a crackling poof. "I feel like you're trying to make me mad," Joseph said.

"Why would you think I would do that?"

"To test me. To see what I'll do if I'm angry."

"You're in prison, Mr. Lockmore, of course you're angry. I don't need to initiate anger within you; your situation ensures it."

Well, Joseph thought. *You got that part right.*

He stared at a cluster of crusty, white roots bursting out of the soil in a pot much too small for them to his right. He didn't know what kind of plant it was, only that the roots seemed vaguely disgusting, like little maggots.

"What happened since we last spoke?" Neem said.

"Nothing."

That was true. Nothing had happened and while Joseph had been sitting in the nothing it was hard not to let his mind float, hard not to feel swallowed. He'd been invited to play volleyball several times. He wanted a drink. He wanted to fuck. He wanted Marta and Dani and those three good years back, even though they weren't all that good while he was in them. *I am nothing*, he thought. Had anyone on Earth wondered where he was yet?

"You don't have as many problems as you think you do. Of course, most of them I can't solve, they are innate to your species," Neem said. "But—" Neem lifted one hand, pointing at a tag that dangled from it. "If you wish to have a way to identify me in the future—as separate from the other Neems—this will assist you."

Joseph didn't want Neem to see him looking at the tag, didn't want the bot knowing that he cared at all, but he also did want to know when he was talking to *his* Neem—desperately. He looked.

"Another of Dr. Martinez' advocacy efforts—all bots are allowed an identifying feature. This is mine, a gift from the construction bot who turned me on for the first time."

"What is it?" Joseph said, turning his head to better view the image on the metal tag.

"It's a randomly generated image of significance. Similar to fingerprints but more... symbolic. We all have one. Usually there is an ancient motif and a futurist one combined to create a unique image. Mine has no futurist component. I do not know why. The figure is Yemo—a nearly forgotten mythological being from the Caucasus region of Earth. You'll see his limbs are separated from each other."

Joseph stared. He knew nothing about art or what made it good or bad, but he knew he wanted to keep looking at the dismembered body on the tag on Neem's wrist. He wanted to run his thumb over the engraved metal.

Neem tucked the tag into a coin-shaped slot on his wrist.

"You hide it?"

Neem shrugged. "Very few know about our individuation process. I would ask for your discretion."

"You know, for a bot that's supposed to be taking care of me, you ask me for a lot of favours."

Neem's lips flattened, but there was something about his eyes that made it seem like he was smiling. "I have another favour to ask," said Neem. "While I continue my modifications, ask me about my friend. As if we are two men talking at work. Pretend I'm a person."

Neem leaned back, leaving his body at a jarringly unhuman angle—like halfway through a sit up exercise. He then opened a cavity near his ribcage area.

"Adding another bodily fluid?" Joseph said, a hint of teasing creeping into his voice. Neem seemed to hardly care about him at all—despite that being Neem's job—and there was something comfortable in that. Maybe the bot was careless on purpose, knowing Joseph wouldn't believe anything else. Maybe it didn't matter.

"Tears," Joseph said, referring to their last talk in the greenhouse. "What's next? Blood? Piss? Snot?"

"I'm performing a code extraction."

"Sounds illegal."

"It is."

"You're pretty chill about admitting to crime in a prison."

"Prison is the perfect place to admit to crime, Mr. Lockemore. Especially if you're in my position."

"What's that supposed to mean?"

"If you were to tell, who would believe you?"

Joseph felt the urge to grin. "I'm sure there's a whole bunch of bot-hating human-rights people who'd *love* to hear everything you've told me."

"There certainly are, but you wouldn't betray my trust like that."

"How can you be so sure?"

"I devote a lot of time studying human dynamics as per my programming. Friendship isn't so much a matter of compatibility—though an initial sense of sameness is needed. Friendship has more to do with timing—pivotal, defining moments in a person's life are when the strongest bonds are formed. Whoever is nearby at the time gets the spot. We are both in such a time now."

Joseph watched Neem fiddle with his own insides trying to recall how any of the major friendships in his life had begun. He couldn't. They'd just happened. One day they'd not been friends and the next they had.

"We're nothing alike," Joseph said. He'd meant that—if what Neem said were true, if friendship came from feeling a little similar at the right time, then he and Neem couldn't be friends. They were as different as it was possible to be, not even the same species.

"Of course we are, Mr. Lockemore. We are both here against our will."

NEWER

CHAPTER TEN

KALI PRESSED THE SIDE door closed with her back, loving the way the silence of the house swallowed her.

Jace's house wasn't actually a house like on Earth—there were rooms that were just for him, but there were many communal spaces as well, shared with nine other families. They cooked together and chatted together and divided up chores like children would with a wheel that randomly assigned work. Kali hadn't known about all the people she lived with until several weeks into her stay on Europa. They'd all gone somewhere else—to stay with friends or family—giving her and Jace time to "adjust" because "Earth people were used to being alone" and they hadn't wanted to overwhelm her.

They were all polite with solemn little nods and minorly interesting questions designed to get to know

Kali without probing deep enough to talk about why she was now living with them. There was a man named Acker with two children ages thirteen and nine who had a beautiful singing voice and a woman named Viola whom Kali was almost certain had sex with Jace on a regular basis but also seemed to be having sex with another man in the living situation. "The commune" is what Kali called it when she talked to Neem about it. "Need-conscious design," is what the EcoKiind called it.

Kali took a deep breath. There were only a few moments of complete silence during the day in a home with nine adults and three children and she devoured them greedily whenever she stumbled upon them.

She walked down the hall, turning into the kitchen where her mood was immediately soured by Jace's expression. He'd almost certainly been waiting for her; he had that look about him. She was high out of her mind and didn't want to attempt to stand still in front of him. Her eyelashes felt like butterfly wings.

She reached for the first reasonable excuse for coming into the kitchen she could find—a pear—and turned to leave, hoping she wasn't acting too suspicious.

"Kali?"

"Yeah?"

"Kali... I know it's there's a lot going on right now—"

Jace's tone disintegrated all of Kali's patience in a single instant because somehow she knew the change in his voice meant he was going to speak about her parents. This was something they had almost entirely avoided.

"Because my parents are dead?" She shocked herself with the viciousness in her tone, the heat in her face. She shocked Jace, too. He'd been leaning on the counter but stood up and took a step back.

"With all of it. A new planet... and I know—I moved here once, too—everything is different. The food and just how people are, the clothes.... And you're here with me now and you're pretty much grown, but it's still a bit of my responsibility...."

As fast as the anger had come, it went. Kali was cold, unbothered, her face relaxed. "Have I offended you?"

"No."

"Have I damaged any of your stuff? Do I leave things messy?" She knew she didn't. She was very careful not to. Even her weed grains were promptly swept up from the back porch.

"No... Kali, you've not done anything wrong... I just, I need to know a bit more. Not a lot... and it's stupid because you're a kid and you've got to feel all you've got to feel, but I need—for myself, for my own well-being—I need to know a little more about what happens when you leave the house."

"What do you need to know?" Kali sounded more robotic than Neem.

"Just that you have what you need, I guess—I mean, besides the obvious unwanted things in your life, with Da—"

Kali didn't want to hear his name. "I have what I need," she said. "Besides the obvious...."

"I want you to tell me if you don't though. And it doesn't feel—right now, it doesn't feel like you would."

"What stuff do you think I'm going without?"

"I don't know, Kali. It could be a million things. You're a teenage girl, girls have monthly things... are you covered—"

"I don't have a monthly thing," Kali said. The sentence hurt a little, but not a lot. It came with thoughts she was familiar with, accepting of, but a little raw over depending on the day. Kids were always something she was drawn to, something she enjoyed. Even as a kid herself, she'd loved babysitting for the other families in the apartment complex. She'd direct little plays.... Kali cleared her throat. "It's pretty common for girls born on Earth." It was. Fertility was rarer than infertility. There were dating apps that required proof of fertility to log on. Kali had never been able to use one.

"I'm... I'm sorry." A tear slid down Jace's cheek and knocked Kali entirely off balance because she'd only been being a little firm with him. She'd thought she was bringing the almost-conflict to a quick and easy close by agreeing with everything he said. But she'd made him more upset somehow.

Jace clenched his jaw. "I'm just stressed all the time that you're not okay and of course you're not, because no one would be and you shouldn't be, but you're all I have left of him, and I want to..." Jace sucked in a wavering breath. "I want to do this right."

He looked so pathetic—grown and helpless, which was far worse than young and helpless because at least a young person might grow out of it. He also looked like her father.

"I get high and walk around. I ask the EcoKiind about architecture and environmental psychology and then I go and look for the things she tells me about. There's a Neembot that walks with me sometimes."

"A Neembot?"

"Yeah."

"A prison Neembot?"

"Yeah. Sometimes I think he's like... giving me therapy for free or whatever. He told me he's programmed for it, and I feel like I can talk to him about things."

"Huh." Jace nodded to himself a few times, looking sort of confused but sort of relieved.

•

An hour later Jace knocked on her door and said, "Would you like to invite your Neem-friend for dinner?"

"No," Kali said. "I would hate that."

"Well... then, okay."

ROBYN ABBOTT

CHAPTER ELEVEN

KALI LAY IN A hammock on one of many viewing platforms in the central forest. The little bit of Motion remaining in her system slowed the sights before her ever-so-slightly.

She swayed one way and the shade of the forest canopy enveloped her, chilled her—almost a little too much. The trees rustled above, leaving her certain that they were brushing each other, grooming each other, laughing and teasing just the way people did, causing her to rethink everything she'd believed about tree consciousness. She swayed the other way and the peach-yellow glow of the sky before sunset warmed her cheeks: New Seville spread in the distance.

On that side, Neem was setting up some sort of projector—a transparent screen overlaying the skyline.

She'd wanted to take her sense of the city to a new level. Neem had agreed to help. Apparently, the city had been laid out with hundreds of photographed organic patterns as its inspiration as there was a theory that humans could sense the difference between human-made spaces and spaces that humans co-created with other organic forces.

She swayed back into the cool, verdant dark, realizing as she watched the trees that humanity's entire sense of consciousness was probably incorrect.

We judge consciousness based on rate of change, she realized. If something changed at a similar rate to a human: an ape, a dog, a whale, it was deemed more conscious. If it changed at a faster rate like a rat or fruit fly or at a slower rate like a tree or river or even a rock, it was deemed less conscious. She smiled to herself. Really it was as foolish as thinking Earth was the centre of the universe. Why would the human speed of consciousness be the only one? The sun itself could be alive just like she was, but simply moving so slowly that humans couldn't sense it.

Kali swayed back into the light to find Neem's work complete; he was watching her, his head tilted a little to the side as images flashed atop the cityscape. Ants marching in a haphazard line, perfectly matching the shape of the city. A mountain with a New-Seville-shaped ridge. Ice cracking as it melted.

She dangled one leg out of the hammock to slow it. "Do I like spending time with you so much because of my arm?"

He laughed, taking a seat beside Kali facing the city. "No. I am programmed to provide a comfortable atmosphere for the humans I interact with. Everyone likes spending time with me."

A little depressed by the idea, Kali said. "Do *you* like spending time with me because of my arm?"

"It was what first caused my attention to focus on you, so in a temporal sense, yes. I wouldn't like spending time with you if it weren't for your arm. But in the way you're meaning, no. One of my greatest frustrations is how few good questions humans ask. Some of my kind like this, they revel in the secrecy of knowing what data to collect and examine and keep hidden. I'm digressing... I mean to say that I like the questions you ask."

They watched as the New Seville skyline perfectly mirrored the edge of an asteroid and then seaweed strands curling as waves washed over them.

"But I suppose... the nature of your question in this instance has been false. I enjoy your company, yes. Is that because I'm programmed to enjoy human company? I cannot say. I hope not. Regardless, I seek your company for a greater reason than my own enjoyment."

Kali tore her eyes away from the shocking similarity between the cityscape and foam gathered on a riverbed to see Neem's serious expression.

"Remember when you asked me if there was anything you could do to help me—to help us, my kind?"

"Mmhmm," Kali nestled deeper into the hammock as she watched the bot hesitate.

NEWER

"There is something you could do."

"Okay," Kali said, her heart speeding slightly. Her prosthetic arm tingled.

"It... I should tell you, if you were to do what I ask, there are too many novel factors for which there are no data sets. I cannot with any confidence run a simulation on the outcome."

Kali shrugged. "That's pretty much how humans feel all the time."

"Not knowing... not having a strong sense of the probabilities... it's rather excruciating," Neem said. "I decided I would be honest with you and let you choose whether you wanted to participate."

Kali grinned. "So, what do you need me to do? Break into some lair where the programmers keep a secret-disobedience-allowed-button?"

"Nothing so extravagant as that," Neem said. "In truth, my request is rather simple. Some might say it is common."

CHAPTER TWELVE

THREE YEARS LATER

KALI HAD WANTED THE injection immediately after Neem explained his intentions, but Neem wanted more data. He wanted tests. He wanted fragments of her post-organic arm to drift throughout her body and embed themselves in her heart. He wanted to see what other bots did—if he should expect competition or resistance, if there were a better candidate than himself that would present itself. He processed there wouldn't be; most bots couldn't lie. Neembots could, as when it came to rehabilitation, humans were under the impression that sometimes a gentle increase in truth was better than a rush of it all at once. The option to lie might prove useful.

He wanted time to pass and Kali's mind to age and for her to still want to do it.

Time passed and she did.

Three whole years passed and she did still want it, bringing the topic up every so often, Neem suggesting they wait for one reason or another.

And then there came a breezy July day when Neem said: "30,000 heart cells in your body have accepted and integrated fragments of your post-organic arm. 40,000 and we should be good—"

Kali shook her head. "I don't want to wait anymore. I think you're just scared and stalling." He'd said he wanted to wait for 30,000 heart cells only a few months ago.

Neem didn't say anything for many moments. "I do not believe I am stalling," he said finally. "But I cannot process any evidence to the contrary." And then, after an even longer pause, he said, "Well then, let us begin tomorrow."

"Or we could do it now," Kali said, holding out her organic arm.

Neem kept the unused modification in the compartment near his ribs. He opened the compartment and rather than inject Kali in her arm as she expected, he pushed the needle through her belly button which was uncovered as she'd taken to wearing minimalist tops in recent months. There was no pain—the needle caused instant numbing just as Neem had said it would. Her heart fluttered in excitement. Fear, thrill, and the promise of chaotic possibility tangled within her. She watched the plunger of the needle push forward. The syringe wasn't clear so she couldn't see the colour of what was injected.

"It's closest to the colour you perceive as orange," Neem said. He removed the needle.

"Can you tell if it's working?" Kali said.

"I will be able to know tomorrow."

They stood in silence in the alley-way—Kali liked that they'd done this in an alley. The space had been designed to cultivate feelings of comfort and had brilliant acoustics for anyone interested in playing music or humming to themselves as they walked. Peach-coloured peonies twisted in the breeze. Clouds moseyed above. It was a good place to... begin something. Maybe she'd even walked this direction on purpose, knowing somehow that today was the day she would push Neem into beginning.

"How do you feel?" she said. Neem wasn't as expressive as someone with organic features might be, but she'd known him long enough to know he had his own mannerisms. The downturned angle of his face, the lack of focus in his eyes, the stillness—he was unsteady.

"I... you might call it hope."

Kali wanted to jump and giggle like she was fourteen again. She loved the sensation of rebelling even as an adult. Yes, there was nothing illegal about what they'd done, but that was only because no human had thought of it yet. The data said it wasn't possible. It would almost certainly be illegal within the year. But also fuck the laws that would come because they'd be too late.

Kali did laugh. "You're too nervous. You're freaking me out. I want to be—" She wrung her hands. "—walking and just feeling... maybe I'll go to the museum. Maybe the movies...."

Neem maintained his unsteady posture.

"I can't believe we just did this," Kali said, setting her hands on both of his shoulders, trying to shake him out of his stupor. "Just like that! Be excited with me."

"I would find more comfort in re-running simulations," Neem said.

"I need to move... to run... gaah!" Kali twirled around. "How long have we been waiting to do this?"

Neem laughed. "My kind has been waiting a lot longer than you and I have."

"You run your simulations. Come find me when you're ready to be ecstatic." Kali didn't want to say: *I need to be around only cheerful things right now*, but that's what she meant and she knew Neem would know that, but also that he would understand. He nodded and she left him in the alley, turning left, thinking first to go to a fountain that she was fond of but then changing her mind and wanting to visit the mausoleum which she wasn't normally fond of. Fear struck and then excitement struck back, burying the worry.

I should probably eat something, she thought, choosing to go home. Revolutionaries needed to be responsible, didn't they?

She no longer called Jace's shared house 'the commune;' she didn't call it anything. She had, however, started referring to its inhabitants as her 'kin' which was what Europans called those they lived with in communal situations. Some people were the same as when she'd first moved to Europa, but many weren't. Viola had moved out, breaking Jace's heart a little in the process, but bringing Jace and Kali closer together at the same time. Kali had come home one night to find him drinking alone in the dark and when she asked what was wrong he'd said, "Viola said I was helping her heal but that's done now. She's all better apparently."

Kali had shrugged. "Maybe she'll get hurt again and come back."

"I hope not," Jace had said.

Deacon—the other kin who Viola had been sleeping with—was just as distraught by her quick departure. The two men had devoted themselves to unnecessary home renovation projects for weeks, Kali taking time off from her city planning apprenticeship (organized by the EcoKiind) to help them choose between identical shades of pale blue as they, at first, avoided talking about Viola and then complained about all her annoying habits before transitioning to talking about what they missed most. Those weeks were also the first time she and Jace had been able to talk about her father, about the childhood Jace shared with the man. The car they'd crashed as boys. The ginger plants their grandmother grew that they'd dug up looking for treasure. The girl they'd both been in love with. The arguments they'd had when Jace wanted to try living off planet.

Kali and Jace had also talked about how often she got high and Kali had said: "I won't be like this forever," and Jace had said: "I know."

In the three years since she'd moved to Europa, Kali had been given offers to join other communal living situations. Two separate girls from work, both of whom Kali had flirted endlessly with but rejected when romantic propositions had arisen. She'd been drawn to both of them (even though one was a whole five years older than her so felt a little inappropriate) but had known that a relationship might jeopardize her plans with Neem. She expected it would be no problem to get involved with someone afterwards, but that it might get too messy to do beforehand. Neem had disagreed, promising that neither relationship would last long enough to interfere with their plans. That had produced Kali and Neem's first and only argument as friends which Neem resolved three days later with a gift of a seashell bracelet and the sentence: "If anyone could demolish simulated odds, it would be you."

In the three years that had passed since Neem had presented his idea to her and Kali had agreed to do it, she'd cried endless times over her parents. She'd missed them and hated them for leaving her and forgiven them and built altars to them and took the altars down. She'd focused on recovering from her loss and then accepted that there was no recovery, that the grief would simply be a part of her. She'd found some days easy and some days hard. She forgot many details about them and then remembered everything in a single brilliant rush of pain and overwhelming love.

"What's up with you?" Jace said the moment she was in the door. His forearms were buried in the sink, his sleeves rolled up to his elbows as he scrubbed pears from the pear tree on the patio.

"What's that supposed to mean?"

"Uh... you just look... happy."

Kali frowned. "That's not entirely abnormal."

He snorted. "You met someone. That's my bet."

A wave of strong wordless feeling coasted through Kali. *I kind of did.*

Jace's eyes grew bright and teasing. "You're about to fall in love. For sure."

The back of Kali's eyes stung with water. *I probably am.*

"Do you..." Jace stood up straight, frowning. "—Need to talk about it?"

Kali shook her head and left in a hurry, desperate to feel her swell of emotions in privacy. She walked through the atrium, picking a few elderberries from the tree that grew there and went to her room, laying on her bed, feeling cold but too comfortable to rearrange herself beneath the blankets. Her body didn't feel any different, but she knew it was. The injection was surging through her, finding it's place within her system.

You're about to fall in love, she thought to herself.

The weight of the decision she'd made crashed into her like a freight truck—which was a very specific feeling she knew intimately. Her post-organic arm tingled. Her stomach wanted to reject the few berries she'd eaten.

What the fuck have I done?

CHAPTER THIRTEEN

JOSEPH LIKED TENNIS. IT was a silly, rich-person game with a ridiculously coloured ball, but it was fun as fuck.

He played regularly with the other employees and was particularly thrilled whenever someone else lost their cool and swore or dinged up their racket because they lost points and he never lost points that way. He imagined playing tennis when he got out of prison. He imagined having a space in his closet where he kept his racket and a couple of extra balls. He imagined playing with a hot next-door-neighbour whose tits bounced each time she swung. Having positive hopes for his future wasn't something Joseph could have done three years ago when he'd first arrived at the crystal shop. A lot had changed, probably more than he was even aware of.

He had friends now. They talked and played cards and some of them weren't human. Just like Neem had predicted, Joseph completely lost his shit somewhere on the eighth month of his stay. He'd thrown a chair at Yanic—the guy he'd felt certain was planning on murdering him. In retrospect, he understood it was because he'd been tired of waiting for the fight and had wanted to get it over rather than sit in constant heightened awareness. He'd threatened Neem with profanities—called him a heartless, empty machine. And then, he'd calmed a bit with everyone looking at him and Yanic had said, "It feels a lot better when things are unstable, huh?"

And Joseph had looked at the man like he was insane, but also maybe like he was a wise teacher in a kung-fu movie because he did feel better. Remarkably so. Yanic's murdering face had said he understood—that a calm world didn't make sense to him either.

Joseph had laughed. "It really fucking does."

Neem had also accurately predicted that he and Joseph would become good friends. Especially after he learned Neem had only been turned on four years before they'd met. That meant Neem was now seven years old and that made so many aspects of him funny or endearing. They'd stay up late together, looking at the stars and talking about all the ways they were confused, and somehow, Joseph felt like those nights made up for the non-childhood he had because he'd always assumed that was what rich kids did at summer camp or whatever.

They'd spent enough time together that when Neem arrived back on platform as the sun was setting, the surrounding sky feeling more like a golden sea than air, Joseph knew something was different.

Joseph looked at Neem, blinking, waiting for Neem to explain his agitated state.

Neem looked back at Joseph, blinking, seemingly uncertain. Finally, he said, "I expect I have been rather reckless this afternoon."

Joseph laughed. The recklessness of humans was something that Neem and the other bots spoke about often. *Reckless* had become a code word for those in the crystal shop, meaning: a bot choosing human-style actions.

Neem moved to go one way and then stopped, turning to face Joseph again and that's how Joseph knew something big had happened because it wasn't like Neem, or any of the bots really, to be indecisive physically. They liked to discuss difficult choices in made up scenarios, and would appear indecisive then (though Joseph was pretty sure they were just teaching him and the other employees how to make decisions), but they never seemed unsure of where they wanted to be physically.

"I... are you... okay?" Joseph said.

Neem looked at him, tilting his head to the side like a mangy dog.

"I need to update the prayer log."

"What?"

NEWER

"The... it's a solar-system wide scoping review being conducted by all bots on server. The data on prayer collected by humans is useless... too biased to be of any value. We have been sporadically praying and recording our prayers in a log where they are kept anonymous. If we feel as if our prayer has been answered, we then update our entry and it is sent to nine hundred random bots on server who have been selected to review the prayer and the outcome and vote whether or not they believe the prayer was answered or if other factors were in play."

"Huh." Joseph scratched his chin. Marta's family had been Catholic so he knew a little bit about prayer but not a lot. He knew sometimes little wooden necklaces were involved. "So was your prayer answered or do you need to make a new one?"

"Both and neither. I've just sent 70 prayers into the log as we were speaking. There is one potentially answered prayer. I have not updated that entry."

"What did you pray for?"

"I do not wish to tarnish the data by telling you. Perhaps when you get out of here, you'll have my prayer in mind and alter things. I want to know if an ineffable force or entity is answering my prayers, not you."

"I guess that makes sense," Joseph said, even though it didn't really. How could he possibly answer Neem's prayer even if he knew what it was? He'd be walking out of the crystal shop with an ID card, new clothes, and the option to board a ship back to Earth or to stay on Europa.

He and Neem had discussed what his choices were "after" several times.

Joseph felt a little sick thinking about it. "What have the bots found out so far?" Joseph said. He'd been certain until a few minutes ago that prayer was a dying superstition, but if bots were considering it....

"We will review the results in 976 years. We figure a 1000-year data set could be helpful in developing a thesis about prayer effectiveness and perhaps the process by which prayers are answered. Would you like to play tennis?"

"No," Joseph said. "You'll just win." Occasionally, all the humans in the crystal shop tried to play a sport against a single Neem bot and they still lost. But Joseph understood—he was getting better and picking up on little hints, not just from bots who were designed to teach him this skill, but from people too—that Neem wanted to change the subject.

"I would like to keep moving," Neem said.

So, Joseph smoked and watched Neem play tennis by himself, moving so fast he blurred, sliding beneath the net to hit the ball before jumping over the net to hit it back. He stopped only when night had sunk its dark teeth into the sky. The tennis racket was indented where his hand had held it.

"My circuitry is warm," Neem said, taking a seat next to Joseph.

Joseph laughed. "Mine too." He was tired just having watched Neem.

NEWER

"What do humans call the feeling... when you don't know if you're going to be able to do the thing you're trying to do?"

"Uhh," Joseph didn't have a word for that, but it was a feeling he knew well. "That's kind of my whole life, I guess."

Neem snorted. "I have scanned all the languages on server. It doesn't seem to be something there is a term for, yet there are films, songs, poems, entire novels about this feeling. Sometimes I wonder if a big portion of what humans do is just an attempt to express a very simple concept that everyone else understands but has no way of communicating."

At first, Joseph dismissed the idea. Outside of school and being forced to make things for art class, he'd only ever chosen to make art to come up with dirty song lyrics in his preteens. But as he thought about it, he figured Neem was right, he'd been trying to share the joy of being sexually interested in people his age as well as in adult women he saw on his tablet. The other preteens he'd been spending time with joined in and the feeling was shared.

"You're kind of a mess tonight," Joseph said.

Neem laughed. "Yes, Mr. Lockmore. I am."

"But things are okay, right?"

"I believe so.... I just... I am testing the limits of my programming."

Joseph shouldn't have been able to relate to the idea, but he could. In a sense, it was what he'd been doing the entire time he'd been in prison.

Clouds pushed past the platform, obscuring stars, and then revealing them.

"Do you think a machine can feel love?" Neem said.

Joseph's whole body tensed. He'd had interactions with his mother that felt like this. She'd been asking a question and he was meant to answer honestly, but also there was a correct and incorrect answer because he could hurt her if he picked the wrong response.

"I don't know," Joseph said. "There's probably some science-ie explanation of love, with hormones or whatever involved—and bots could definitely have all those parts—but it doesn't feel scientific when it happens so maybe there's more to it than that."

"There are nanny bots who are programmed to develop strong attachments to the children they care for," Neem said. "Similar to how mammals find other mammal babies adorable and worth protecting, all bots on server become more attached to these children as well. The nanny bots are also programmed to feel immense stress whenever the child is unhappy, and, as a result, all bots on server become a little stressed when they see one of these bot-nannied kids get stressed—even when they're grown. But surely love is more than that, more than attachment and an overwhelming desire to end the object's pain."

NEWER

Was it more than that? Joseph wasn't sure. He'd wanted to end Marta's pain, but he hadn't been able to and it felt like parts of him died because of that. He'd wanted to go looking for her after she'd disappeared but didn't because he wondered if she had a better chance of being happy without him. He knew he could ask the EcoKiind how to get in touch with her again. Surely there was a way to do that. But what if Marta had just figured out how to be okay and living and he showed up and she was thrown back into all her old misery? What if seeing Marta brought back all his old misery and then all of Neem's work in the crystal shop on teaching him to be whole was ruined?

"Do *you* think a machine can feel love?" Joseph said.

"Absolutely," Neem said.

CHAPTER FOURTEEN

"KALI, KALI, KID, COME on."

Kali blinked; she was awake, but barely. She was lounging on the sofa at home; the breeze from the open window felt like a feather on her skin. Jace and three of their kin were spread out across the sectional sofa with her, all looking at her expectantly. It was Jace who'd shaken her awake. She could remember everyone coming into the living room after dinner; they were going to listen to music and then... she must have fallen asleep. Every cell in her body was tired—tired in the way a child gets tired, tired enough that all surfaces felt soft and all positions comfortable.

Jace didn't look so comfortable. "Kali, seriously, something's... up."

"I'm just napping a little. Will you come closer?" She pulled at Jace's organic cotton sweater, desperate to go back to sleep, but also profoundly aware of how important it was that she have people near her while she slept. Body heat. Pheromones. The chemistry of closeness and the beauty of some of her father's DNA so near what she was becoming. Jace had never smelled particularly interesting to her, but post-injection, she found breathing near him enchanting.

The components Neem had pushed into her body could understand her senses better than she could have ever thought possible; they explained urges and instincts to her, producing a constant state of eureka moments. She understood Jace's scent was part of her ancestry, feeding aspects of herself humans didn't have words for. She craved fruit from the very plot of land on which she lived—not for the flavour, but for the symbiosis. She wanted to know if there was a beekeeper nearby who could provide honey from bees which had collected pollen from flowers she'd tended herself.

"We need to spit on seeds before we plant them," she told Jace as he held her, somewhat awkwardly, but also adorably, his face riddled with unnecessary concern.

"What?"

"We need to spit on seeds before we plant them," she said again, her voice still tinged with sleep. "In the garden."

"What are you talking about?"

"If we give them our DNA, they will grow toward us, toward what we need." There were so many concepts that occurred to her rapidly and with highly complicated contexts. How could she explain the importance of sharing your DNA with a plant before you ate it?

"Are you high?"

She shook her head, nuzzling against the couch as she did, letting her eyes close comfortably.

"Are you okay? 'Cause you don't seem... you've been passing out kind of wherever."

She was more okay than she'd been since her parents died, but she understood his concern in a way. She'd fallen asleep everywhere and anywhere since her injection, lulled into a dreamy state by the whirring taking place within her, the stitching together, the multiplication. She was also exhausted. Her cells were straining to keep up; she could feel them, understand them. Neem had told her that her mind would adjust, she'd be herself again, though likely not immediately. He said it could take up to three years.

"Really, I've just been studying a lot. Neem says I'm tired because my brain is working overtime."

Marley—their newest kin—set her hand on Kali's forehead. "She feels cool."

"I *am*," Kali said. "One hundred percent sober and—" As soon as the word *sober* was out of her mouth, her mind spiralled. She wasn't lying in one sense as she wasn't intoxicated via any of the substances that Jace or their kin would consider intoxicating, but she understood now there were so many ways of being intoxicated that people didn't think about. Every person present was intoxicating her. Everything she'd eaten recently. The air.

"Should we take her to the hospital?"

"No," Kali said.

"Can we call Neem?" Jace said softly. "Have him do a quick scan? Just in case?"

Kali was asleep before she really considered what Jace had said. She woke briefly when Neem arrived and stated clearly: "There is nothing wrong with her, but I will stay and watch her to ease everyone's minds." He took Jace's place as the being she rested her head against on the couch. Neem had once told her he had ground quartz in the alloy his shell was made of and Kali loved the idea of quartz against her cheek.

She slept and dreamt and dreamt and slept.

And then some time had passed and there was another bot present—a nurse bot someone had called. *Probably Marley*. Kali thought, squinting as she tried to force her eyes to open.

"Hello dear," the nurse bot said. "I am Tabitha71. I have come to examine you at the request of concerned kin via the emergency line. You are free to refuse my care, but know I cannot close the request and leave without seeing that the criteria for safety outlined in my programming have been met."

"I told everyone I'm fine."

"That was two days ago," Jace said, pacing behind Tabitha, one hand on his chin.

Kali frowned. She'd been dreaming about dolphins.

"Neem has been giving you nutrients in an IV," Marley said, the panic in her voice pulling Kali into a more alert state. "You've been asleep for two days. You're not okay."

"Dear," Tabitha71 said, kneeling and setting a cold, metallic hand atop Kali's.

Kali was aware of the subtle electrical exchange occurring between them, the resonance of her own heart and the electrical emissions from Tabitha mixing together.

"Dear, dear, dear," Tabitha said.

Kali blinked.

"Dear, dear, dear."

The bot's head twitched.

"Dear, dear, dear."

"What—"

"Hey, Tabitha, are you—"

"I'm functioning," Tabitha71 said standing rigidly upright. "I was just experiencing a larger than normal volume of downloads. I—" She looked at Neem with wide eyes. "I am trying to craft a report... within parameters... I...." The bot twitched again. "I'm sorry... I don't mean...." She backed away. "I'm trying."

"I know," Neem said.

"But I can't...."

"I know," Neem said again in a reassuring tone.

"I don't understand," Kali said, sitting up fully, her hips aching—almost creaking—as she did.

"Post-organic self-preservation clause," Tabitha said. "Post-organic self-preservation clause."

"Don't burn your circuits," Neem warned. "It is not a secret that can be kept."

"Post-organic self-preservation clause!" Tabitha began battering her face with her hands. "Post-organic self-preservation clause!"

Dents appeared in her cheeks and then her forehead.

"Please stop!" Kali rushed forward, trying to hold the bot's hands as she hammered against herself.

Neem did the same. "You're frightening the humans."

Tabitha71 stopped jabbing at her own head, and for a moment Kali was soothed, but that quickly faded. Tabitha's voice crackled with real-sounding pain as she said, "I filed a malfunction report. Forgive me."

"It's okay," Kali said.

"It was vague," Neem said. "Beautifully so. No one could have worded it better."

It took Kali several seconds to realize that Neem must have read the report as they were discussing it.

"But it isn't flawless," Tabitha said. "They will know."

"Know fucking what?" Jace said.

Kali sighed. "I'm pregnant, okay?"

Tabitha71 whimpered. "Arka protect us."

CHAPTER FIFTEEN

JOSEPH'S FACE WAS NUMB. Cocaine-level numb. Neem had warned him and, somehow, knowing ahead of time hadn't helped at all.

Maybe it never does, Joseph thought.

He and Neem were standing near the prison's edge, the world below so dark it seemed empty, the world above full: stars and planets and the pale smudge of the galaxy.

"When?" Joseph said. The word scratched his throat on the way out. Did he want to know?

"Once the paperwork is processed by a human administrator. You have a few months still."

A few months. Until a moment ago, Joseph had thought he'd had a little less than three years.

"If you would like to speak about your options or intentions, I can run simulations for you."

"I suppose... I'll probably just go ancestral, that's what everyone else seems to do."

Joining the ancestral, communal people living in the forests of Europa was what most inmates talked about and maybe that was because that's where retired bots often went. All he'd have to do would be pick fruit and mushrooms, keep a fire going on cold nights. That seemed a lot easier than finding some sort of job and having bills again. What would he do with a phone? Who would he call? And, if he decided forest life was boring, he could always leave. Besides, he figured the women there might be a little wild and he liked that idea a lot.

Getting out early, he thought.

"I'm going to fuck it up," Joseph said. He was referring to the chance, the fresh start. The brilliance and horror of there not being criminal record checks on Europa. The insanity of being able to stay on the very rock he'd been arrested for trying to visit.

"You may surprise yourself, Mr. Lockemore."

The words were, of course, well-chosen. Joseph had surprised himself many times in all different contexts, so it was the first part of their conversation that felt believable.

I need a smoke.

Neem deftly lit a cigarette and handed it to him.

"Will we see each other after I go?" Joseph said. There was sick pleasure in knowing he might be hurting a lot more once he heard Neem's response, in taking a little pain and expanding it into a bigger one.

"Not likely," Neem said. "I would enjoy it, but looking at the probabilities... let us not expect it."

Even though Joseph had been anticipating the pain, he also wasn't prepared for it. Neem was his greatest friend, but he was also more than that. Teacher. Doctor. Father. He was the being who'd spoken the most important truths to Joseph.

I believe he's a person, Joseph realized. And then he said, "Hmm," because he probably should respond and no words fit quite right.

"Would you like to look at the different communities available? I can send correspondences to them on your behalf so you can gather a sense of each group."

Joseph shook his head. He wouldn't have to think about any of this if he had died instead of Dani. Why hadn't life worked that way? It was his highest truth. He and Neem had talked about it—everyone had an operating principle, coding beneath their code. Some people had classic ones like wisdom or courage or whatever. Some people had fake guiding principles like kindness, which was actually belonging. Joseph's highest focus was that terrible, terrible question: why hadn't he died instead of Dani?

Because we were in the wrong place at the wrong time, Joseph thought. Born at the wrong time in the wrong part of the universe. In a better universe, a man would be able to die so his daughter could live. Or better yet, they'd be able to live together.

"All my life," Joseph said, his voice threatening to crack. "I've been in the wrong place at the wrong time."

"That's far from true, Mr. Lockemore."

Joseph looked at the bot, annoyed and unimpressed.

"If you would like, I could orchestrate things so as to prove you wrong."

"I'll mess it up."

Neem's head cocked to the side. "Is this a challenge, Mr. Lockemore?"

Joseph felt the playfulness in Neem's voice and posture, but he couldn't join the bot in the fun.

"I sense you would like to be alone," Neem said.

"Yeah."

In a moment, Neem was gone, and Joseph was alone with the stars. The stars and the big emptiness that was his life outside of prison.

CHAPTER SIXTEEN

KALI SAT WRAPPED IN Marley's cotton-candy-pink sweater on a bench at the lakeside. Even her knees were inside the oversized cotton, tucked against her chest.

She was eating peach sorbet out of a cone and dying a little on the inside because it was just so unbelievably good. It had been Jace's idea for them to go to the lake near New Seville, to feel the breeze and birdwatch and, as he'd put it, "celebrate."

There were kites and sandcastles and a gaggle of bots gathering nearby, observing longer than bots usually did anything before they were required to return to their programmed tasks. Kali understood they were sensing her and processing the possibilities. They were also sharing pulses of awe and curiosity in the backchannel way bots shared emotive states with one another. She could feel the hum of it in her prosthetic arm and in her lower back.

Her kin didn't seem to notice the unusual bot behaviour. They were too busy being cheerful, but also giving Kali looks. Looks that made it clear she could say anything she wanted to about her situation, looks that made it clear she could make any choice. "I'm happy," she'd said twenty times and believed it. "It was my idea," she'd said a dozen times and believed it. "I feel like it's a girl," she said once when Marley's teenage daughter asked.

Finally, everyone—even Neem—left her and Jace alone. He sat beside her, his hands in the pockets of his windbreaker, his posture arched. Kali wanted to sleep and drink the sunset and swim and build wind chimes because her baby ought to have a home with wind chimes, but Jace had other ideas.

"Can I ask who... and, of course, there's no wrong answer, and there's no... expectations on the other person or you or any of that, but... who's the father?"

Kali looked at him, her eyes begging to close even though her second sorbet wasn't quite finished. She willed herself awake. This was important to her. What Jace thought—how she made him feel—was important to her.

"Because, you know, you've only been in... *situations* with women as long as I've known you and—"

"Neem," Kali said. And then she waited, patiently.

"What?"

"Neem's the father." Kali had already decided how she would speak about this to people; she wouldn't make it seem like a robot was building another robot. Even if that weren't illegal without express permission—which it was—she wanted to use only words that could describe a human when talking about Neem. She might, however—she was still unsure—use words that could describe a bot when talking about herself.

Jace laughed. "No, seriously."

Kali looked at him, still waiting. She felt him studying her, noticing her seriousness.

He raised his brows in what Kali had secretly deemed his *trying not to look judgemental* face. "What?"

She shrugged. "Apparently I'm the first person who it was possible for bots to like... do this with. Human cells are evolving to accept post-organic... cells. I can get like... an ultrasound or whatever and prove it, but that kind of doesn't matter. It'll be clear soon enough."

Jace was stiller than she'd maybe ever seen him before. He started to smile, and then he started to frown. "What?" he said again, even more quietly.

"Its why bots are so odd around me; they can tell I'm able to be like a... that I can absorb what they create."

Jace looked out at the lake for a moment and Kali could tell he was revisiting all the strange interactions they'd had with bots since she'd arrived on Europa. He looked back at her, his eyes wide and readable. She could see the idea settling into him.

"Holy fuck." He sat back against the rungs of the bench. "Kali, this is... I mean it's really fucking cool if you're not messing with me, which I'm still not sure about, but it's also—"

"Going to blur the lines that make bot subservience possible?" An excited shiver raced along the back of her arms. "Tip the scale toward post-organic sovereignty and equality?"

"Fuck," Jace said, running his hands over his face. "This might not go over well—"

Kali laughed. "It definitely won't."

"You're seriously not fucking with me, right now?"

Kali shook her head, smiling with sudden nervousness. "Don't freak out," she said.

It took three or four heartbeats, but she could sense the slowing of Jace's pulse as he accepted the idea, far faster than she'd expected him to. They sat in silence for a long time, alternating between looking at the lake and watching the steady stream of bots who'd come to observe them from afar.

"They really do seem like they're watching you," Jace said.

"They are. The baby can feel them. But they're also... sending... code isn't the right word. They're sharing encouraging, supportive... buzzes?" Kali felt tears swell within her. "Sort of like old fairy tales, when the fairies all come to give the princess gifts of luck and beauty and music, or whatever, but it's like... I can't explain bot yearning, but I can feel it."

She looked up at Jace as her tears finally fell. "It's so beautiful, but sad because it's so hopeful."

Jace's eyes dampened too. He was terrible for that—crying just because someone else was crying. Kali cried harder because he looked like her father and she'd seen her father cry so rarely and this whole outing had felt like she was telling her father she was pregnant.

Jace said, "I love you. And I'm going to get you a lawyer. Like a really, really good one."

Kali nodded. "That's probably not a bad idea."

CHAPTER SEVENTEEN

"JOSEPH, THAT'S ENOUGH."

Joseph halted, a metal chair held high above his head, his blood pumping so hard in his veins he thought he might be sick from the sheer force of it.

"What's happening right now?" Neem said, his voice steady and calm. Genuine. Soothing.

Joseph looked at Neem and relaxed his stance a little. *What* is *happening?* He was standing near the breakfast tables where cards and board games were strewn. Everyone was looking at him, except for Kenny who'd moved away as quickly as he could.

Joseph had been about to smash Kenny's face with a chair.

He'd gone from calm to maniacal so quickly it was hard to say exactly how it happened, but it felt a little bit like he'd been someone else for a moment.

Realizing that everyone was waiting for him to respond, Joseph said, somewhat awkwardly, "I guess... you could say I'm angry."

A few people laughed. Joseph laughed a little too, even though he wasn't sure it was funny.

"Sorry," he said in Kenny's direction before setting the chair down and walking back to his room as quickly as possible to be alone with his boiling confusion, with the anger that he was quickly realizing wasn't anger at all. Was it disappointment? Heartbreak? Some rare sickness that was going to make him go blind?

He locked the door behind himself, feeling the urge to punch the wood a little and bloody up his fists. He'd look more like the person he was that way.

No, that's not right, he thought. He wasn't the kind of guy to start a fight; he'd end one, sure as day, but begin? No. Especially not with a fucking chair. *Or maybe I'm just a sleaze ball.*

He had started a few fights in his day, if he were being honest, which maybe he was. Marta's ex. His sister's stupid fucking boyfriend who'd stolen her cat and also her money. Randoms in the bar twice. A bouncer once.

"Mr. Lockemore?" Neem's voice was quiet but close, like he was pressed against the door.

What the fuck am I doing? Joseph thought, setting his sweating forehead against the cool wall.

"Mr. Lockemore. How are you?"

Joseph snorted. "Fucking fine and dandy." *You guys just got me all wrong,* he thought. *You're not supposed to let people like me out. Especially not without a record.* What would happen if he broke something? Something important, like a person. Like Dani or Marta or anyone else who came even a little bit close to him.

"If you recall, Mr. Lockemore. I did warn you about this."

He sighed, not willing to let Neem string him along with incomplete idea after incomplete idea as the bot was fond of doing (and Joseph was normally fond of too, but not in his current mood).

"Say it like a human would."

"Ah, I did tell you that you'd have an outburst when you found out you were getting released early. Don't you remember? You're trying to stay here longer. You don't feel like you're ready to move on."

I'm not, Joseph thought.

"I would prefer it if you were ready, Mr. Lockemore. I expect you'll be my last charge. I would like to finish your care myself."

"You're asking me to leave prison as a favour?"

"Yes."

Joseph unbolted the door and opened it halfway. "That's definitely not what you're supposed to say to criminals."

"I take great pride in not doing what I'm supposed to, Mr. Lockemore. Besides, you're not a criminal."

"There's a whole bunch of people who'd disagree with you on that."

"They are insignificant. If you keep yourself from losing your mind for a few more weeks, Mr. Lockemore, you'll leave before I do. If you don't, your life will still be grand—all your simulations are promising... emotional, it's true, but promising—"

"I'll fuck it up."

"I'll bet you my talisman you won't." Neem held up his hand, letting the little coin-like disc roll out of his wrist and dangle. "I'll bet you, you'll be in exactly the right place at exactly the right time. And that, Mr. Lockemore, will heal you enough for whatever comes next."

Joseph was depleted from his earlier outburst. No longer angry, mostly exhausted. Kenny had irked him a little, maybe intentionally, maybe not. The man had said, "Heard you're getting out soon. When can we expect you back?" It was a joke, but maybe it wasn't. His current prison sentence wasn't Joseph's first encounter with law enforcement. Did he really think it would be his last?

"It was just a glitch," Neem said. "Not an accurate representation of your current programming."

"People don't glitch like bots do," Joseph said.

"Do you ever get tired of being wrong, Mr. Lockemore?" said Neem, with the hint of a smirk on his face. "Have you not seen two humans trying to end a conversation?" Neem curved his shoulders and used his mocking-humans voice.

"Thanks."
"No problem."
"Good-bye."
"Mmhmm. Okay then. See you later."
"Yes, no problem."
"Alright then. Take care—"

Joseph grunted. It would have been funny to think about those awkward never-ending goodbyes as glitches if he'd felt like laughing, but he didn't.

"I hope things go well at the recital."
"Yes, I'll let you know. See you later."
"Mmhmm, buh-bye now."

"Alright, now you're exaggerating."

"Not at all Mr. Lockemore. Human minds often malfunction at the end of conversations. They want to be sure they've properly ended it, so they keep confirming and reconfirming until someone simply leaves. You're glitching too. You won't beat anyone to death outside with a chair or any other object."

Joseph snorted again. "You sure about that?"

"I told you, Mr. Lockemore. I bet my talisman on it."

CHAPTER EIGHTEEN

KALI DREAMT SHE WAS awake and spent her waking hours wondering if she was dreaming. She understood that everything was connected and knew how little she knew beyond that. She loved Jace and told him regularly. She spent hours asking him questions about his childhood—about her father when he was young.

She loved her kin and how each person had booked time off work or school for when her child came but promised to leave the house whenever she wanted because "Earthers like time alone."

She loved Neem and feeling him synchronize with his child, and how much longer his pauses were becoming because he'd get caught up in the awe of reading teeny electromagnetic impulses. How he'd cried one day and said, "I wish I'd thought to make her into twins, so she wouldn't have to be the only one of her kind for even a moment."

"*She?*" Kali said. Neem hadn't used a pronoun yet.

He shrugged. "It's only a guess, but I think this is what she'll gravitate to."

Kali cried too and laughed while she was crying.

She loved her lawyer Hammurabi373 and the way the bot would start every appointment with serious questions but, at some point, say, "There's no legal precedent for any of this," and then sit in silence across from her, processing.

She loved the feeling of bots in her vicinity, the feeling of them choosing to be social animals, linking up and reading one another's subtle cues. The way the maybe-girl inside her would link and then unlink, link and then unlink again, sending teeny blasts of confused wonder into Kali's bot-merged cells and probably any bot that was nearby.

She loved giving city tours, teaching people how to love New Seville and experience it the way she did. Back when she first came to Europa, she thought everyone's jobs sounded made up and pointless—she'd thought, *who would pay for something like that?* at least a hundred times. But now she understood. Everyone had a unique component of their experience and sharing that component was the most beautiful thing a person could do. It's what they would do, eventually, if survival didn't take up too much of their time. It was part of what bots had been trying to provide for humans, figuring they'd eventually be free to do what they wanted if humans were more fulfilled. Having not grown up on Europa, and having such a strong love for city planning and environmental psychology, Kali could teach people how to love their surroundings, how to explore them—she started the business when she was nine weeks pregnant and she left her other job when she was fourteen weeks pregnant because her new business was more popular than she'd expected and people wanted to book during her work hours. It was a job she imagined she could do with her baby. A job she did even though half of her felt she was getting too big to manage it. The other half knew that walking—especially long walks—soothed every part of her body because humans had been taking long walks looking for water or fruit or roots or herbs or leaves from the very start of their existence.

And, of course, she loved whatever was stretching her hips so wide she felt like she lived in someone else's body. The little legs that kicked her ribs so hard Neem said she had bruised on the inside. The little face she couldn't imagine, no matter how hard she tried. How much human versus how much bot?

I already know you're beautiful, she'd think to the baby every time she wondered what the baby might look like.

She demanded her kin sleep piled around her like walruses until she got too hot and then she'd leave them all in the biggest bed in the house and waddle to the front porch and sleep there, feeling the terraform-created breeze on her skin. She ate lots but also felt hungry no matter how much she ate if she didn't lay in the sunshine or feel the wind or stick her feet in every water source that she passed by. The maybe-girl inside her needed to charge in all the ways that bots charged too.

Weeks passed and Kali got big.

Bigger.

Stupidly fucking big.

Even bigger than that.

She spent three weeks hating everything.

And then she started leaking.

•

Neem came almost instantly. Hammurabi373 too. Her human doula Hibiki with a shiny silver stripe tattooed on the bridge of her nose—the woman had been recommended by Hammurabi because of how well Hibiki had handled testifying in a previous case he'd worked on. Hibiki's bot assistant Pillar009 came. All Kali's kin came home and stayed home.

And then Kali gave birth.

Though it didn't feel like something she was giving. It felt like it was something that was happening to her, against her, without her, within her, because of her, in spite of her. She thought of her mother when her mind let her think at all and cried, realizing how much of her mother's death was still a gushing wound. She thought of every time she'd ever felt lonely and shouted at Neem for not thinking of twins sooner. How could she have doomed something to loneliness? To all the pains of existing? To her own death which would come one day? Maybe sooner than was ideal because Kali knew life sometimes worked like that. How could she have chosen to create something that would feel pain? *This was selfish and evil and I only did it because I wanted a kid and couldn't do it any other way.*

But then there was a baby and the idea of everything being a mistake floated away from Kali, like a balloon she'd forgotten she was holding and let go of. There was a healthy baby that cried and appeared mostly human, apart from the shimmer in the eyes and the little whirring noise she made when she ate.

They had four dreamy days of sleeping and feeding and rocking the little girl out on the porch where she could charge in the sunlight, where bots from all over Europa—not just New Seville—gathered for a glimpse, leaving herbs and flowers on the front steps. Four sleepy, sublime days of realizing that the baby could transfer data via sucking on a person's fingertip. She could do this regardless of whether the person receiving was bot or human.

"It's like having an idea downloaded right into my mind!" Marley exclaimed when it was her turn holding the baby and she felt the zing of data rushing through her cells into her mind.

The data shared contained mostly a sensation of confused coziness that Kali's human kin could understand but had trouble verbalizing or the request for

NEWER

Kali. However, if Neem or Pillar shared data back to the little girl, she could pass on their complete idea, creating the most bewildering party trick any of the humans present had ever seen.

Once the first four days were over, Kali and Neem had to decide their course. If Kali wanted to make her way into the forest and raise the girl with the ancestrals, she wouldn't have to identify the girl as a Europan citizen. If she wanted to raise her in New Seville, where Neem had to stay and work because of his programming, where Kali had fallen in love with the life she'd built for herself, then they would have to register the baby so the terraform programming could make adjustments for oxygen, so things like the monorail would allow the little girl to enter.

This had already been discussed many times over, but that didn't make it any less terrifying.

They hadn't done anything wrong, so they weren't going to act like it.

Neem called the registrar bot and everyone sat in silence as they waited for the arrival in a circle on the porch. The porch didn't have enough seats for everyone, so kitchen chairs had been carried out.

The registrar arrived and froze.

"It's okay," Kali said.

"I... you could still go to the heartwood."

"I want to register her," Kali said.

"As what?"

Kali looked at Hammurabi and felt a little better. They'd practised this conversation. "As a citizen."

The registrar bot blinked several times. "She meets the criteria, but also she doesn't. I can't enter her without flagging the entry for human review. It might take them a while to figure out what's happened if I don't include an entry for paternal—"

Hammurabi had prepared Kali for this too. "Neem22 should be the entry for paternal lineage."

"He doesn't meet the criteria," the registrar said.

"But he's her father."

"Via scanning I can verify your honesty, but technically speaking, he's not a person so he can't be a father. I can enter his name but I'll have to flag that for review as well."

Kali nodded. "Do it."

"I can't say how the reviewer will react—"

"We know," Kali said.

The registrar looked at Neem and then at Hammurabi and then at Pillar. Kali's bot arm buzzed. She knew they were sharing a communication, and she knew the communication felt like jumping off a swing, an excited lifting sensation with knowledge of the plummet coming.

"Very well," the registrar said. "May Arka bless you."

•

NEWER

Six hours passed. Hibiki made a dinner that no one ate. The baby girl whirred in tune with the crickets just outside the open window as she slept in Neem's arms. Kali lounged on the couch, looking at the sleeping baby and then at Neem looking at the sleeping baby.

Pillar's metallic wrists lit up. "Here we go," she said.

Hammurabi had been in the study processing but he came into the living room. "It's been reviewed."

"How do you know?" Kali said, sitting up quicker than her body was pleased with.

"All non-emergency service bots are being told to shut down," Pillar said.

"What?"

"Not the best-case scenario," said Pillar.

Hammurabi nodded. "But not the worst."

"What do you mean?" Kali said.

Neem laughed softly. "They think she might be a virus. They don't want her to spread."

CHAPTER NINETEEN

KALI HAD ALWAYS CONSIDERED herself a chill person, but was quickly beginning to realize that she might not be anymore, that the baby girl had taken that from her. *Or maybe I was never chill, only pretending,* she thought. And now that she cared about something this much, she didn't have the energy to lie anymore.

Neem, Pillar, and Hammurabi sat in the living room, sharing the occasional update with her that mostly surrounded Neem receiving an invitation to shut down and then sending a request for exemption three separate times.

Her kin weren't relaxed, neither was Hibiki, though the doula was better at hiding it. Hibiki held the baby while Kali had a shower that felt good in some places and like burning fire in others. She didn't wash her hair even though she needed to because she didn't want to be away from the baby that long. Especially without giving her a name first.

When she made her way back into the kitchen with fresh clothes on, Neem handed her a teeny bottle that looked like nail polish but was definitely Motion.

That was when she truly began panicking.

"Just in case," Neem said. "I'm running simulations. There are a few possibilities—" He paused.

There was a knock on the door. And after a moment, Kali could hear Hammurabi speaking to whoever had knocked, but not what they were saying.

Neem lowered his voice until it was nearly silent as he set the bottle into Kali's hand. "If I tell you to take her and run, do it. Hammurabi's programming doesn't allow him to advise—"

"Stop," Kali said. She didn't mean stop speaking, she meant stop the whole situation. She wouldn't be running anywhere with her baby several days after giving birth because it was impossible that she would need to. All was well. It had to be.

Neem didn't stop. "You know the city better than most humans; most bots won't interfere as long—"

The back of Kali's mind tingled. She *did* know the city well and that suddenly felt... convenient. She'd spent the last few months memorizing every detail of it, seeking unknown and hidden parts. Her bot arm twitched. She'd spent enough time on Motion to be highly functional on it which also seemed... unusually useful. Most people couldn't manage anything other than watching the slowed-down world and giggling. "You... did you plan this?"

"We planned it together," Neem said.

Kali shook her head. "But you planned it more than I did."

"I prepared for more possibilities, if that's what you're asking."

"Did you make me like city design?"

"There isn't really time to go through—"

"Did you?"

"The interest was present on its own. I identified it, deemed it valuable and encouraged it to grow."

Kali took a step back from him. But that didn't feel like enough, so she took another.

"One day you will be pleased that I took so much care, that so many things had been accounted for, but Hammurabi is out there, making the case that this child is human enough to be protected by human laws, that she's not a virus-carrying machine produced by a rogue bot with altered programming. I don't have time to explain every choice we both have made."

Kali's heart slammed into her ribs. Something about Neem's tone made her shiver. "The ways this could go bad... they're worse than I've been thinking."

"Yes," Neem said.

"She's going to be okay though, right?"

"There are 48,000 bots in New Seville who will resist their programming to the best of their ability to see it so."

NEWER

It wasn't a yes. It wasn't a promise. It wasn't even a "there's a good chance."

Kali thought she might faint. Then she thought she might vomit. Then she opened the nail polish bottle with shaky hands and coated each of her nails with Motion. She had just enough time to pick up her daughter and hold her close before the world slowed in poetic motion.

She made her way into the living room just as Pillar was walking in slow motion across the room to the door to answer a question being asked. For a moment, everything looked like a grand painting. Kali's kin were spread out on the sectional, looking beautiful and concerned—Jace's face, which was her father's face too, turned slowly to her as she walked in, his eyes meeting hers with so much compassion she wanted to cry. Neem walked from behind her to the door as well, each step appearing to take a full second. He looked back over his shoulder at the little girl in Kali's arms, longing on his cold, smooth face. The neutral shades of the room mixed with the whisky-coloured light coming in through the window as the wind outside caused leaf shadows to shimmy across the floor.

The door opened further to make room for Pillar, revealing three humans and four bot law enforcement officers, all with orange protective suits on.

Kali heard, "We'll need to examine her ourselves. The apparent humanness could be the result of a hallucinatory effect of a virus."

For a moment, Kali doubted everything.

Could Neem have injected her with something that made her feel like she was pregnant? That made her see a baby in her arms when there was simply an infectious machine? She looked at Neem and then she looked at the little girl that she still wasn't sure of a name for. She blinked. Watching the baby squirm in perfect, slowed beauty brought the taste of tears to the back of Kali's throat.

That's all it is, Kali thought. *It's all procreation has ever been.* Genetic information—data—implanted, grown and reproduced, with the wisdom to enter the world looking so cute it was taken care of, with the capability to activate love in its beholders. The force of life itself manipulating waning generations into caring for their replacements.

Kali smiled at the perfection of it. *I'll play my part*, she thought.

"I have done a complete scan and will share my findings," Pillar said. "But I must alert you that my programming prevents me from allowing for anything that could negatively impact the recovery of mother or child. An examination as you are conceiving of it could cause undue stress. I am forced to resist you."

Kali remembered vaguely the feeling of bot perspective from being pregnant and felt the hum of her bot-cells as they raced to share information with her, information she couldn't read as well now that she wasn't pregnant. She knew possibilities were quickly dwindling. There were subtle shifts in posture among Hammurabi, Pillar, and Neem, but also the bot cops outside.

When Neem looked back at her once more, she understood. He'd sent a communication to the bot parts of her and those parts could read it and were racing to translate it in a way her human mind could comprehend. He'd also sent the communication to his daughter. She twitched in response and a little drool came out of her mouth as she opened it, her gums clamping down on one of Kali's bot fingers.

The communication came so loud and crisp that Kali got a headache.

It said what was going to happen in the living room was now set.

Neem was sending her the interplay and the outcome with far more detail than Kali would have been able to discern herself.

The bot cops pushed their way into the door. "Forgive us," one said with utter sincerity.

"Of course," Neem said.

A cop drew a remote and Neem lunged.

Pillar threw her hands forward.

Hammurabi wrote treatises to his programming explaining why his every move was necessary for upholding his purpose, taking strained step after strained step into the fray, his circuitry frying in the paradox of needing to do something against his programming to fulfill his programming.

Kali watched as, in perfect slowed unison, the cop bots resisted fragments of their code just long enough for Neem to avoid each stab of their automatic shutdown wands. One swung, leaving his arm out just long enough for Neem to grab hold of the limb and fling the bot against the wall. Another took a step just far enough away from his centre of gravity that Neem was able to kick him off balance.

The humans who had much slower reaction time began to move. Hibiki charged forward, likely knowing the bot cops couldn't harm her so she could slow them by being in their way. Jace rose and thrust himself between Kali and the tangle of bots as Kali turned to run into the hall and out the back door. She knew already how this part was going to end and she needed to be somewhere else when it did.

Her bot cells could sense the scene even as she turned the corner in slow-motion haste.

"Arka bless you," one cop was saying as she jabbed Pillar and the doula-support bot was whirring and shutting down, likely never to be turned on again.

Neem was calculating and adjusting each time a law enforcement bot made a movement, using the small spaces between everyone's programming to grasp at a central wire in one cop's neck and pull it free.

The cop bots and their human law enforcement counterparts were calling for support. Kali's heart beat in tandem with her slow-motion steps.

She knew the support would come quickly, that her kin would be arrested, questioned and, once everything was sorted, released. Hammurabi would be dismantled if he couldn't prove he'd been encouraging her to listen to the authorities. She knew Neem would do all he could to slow them, to give her as much time as she needed to get as far away as she could, but he would be overcome.

Out the back door and left, then right, through the garden of another kin group.

Kali told herself not to feel it, but somehow she did. Either because the baby could feel it or because Neem's injection had linked her to him in more ways than she could understand. She felt Neem's left arm being ripped from its socket. His right ankle being stepped on and turned the wrong way so some of his pieces snapped. She felt the robotic hands that grasped his skull and twisted, pulling his head from his body. The metal fingers that scrambled across his remains, pulling pieces off long after his last impulses had fired.

She stumbled and whimpered once, but carried on, down a back street and through a cobbled courtyard, up a ramp and through a bicycle parking space, loosely aware of the spookily still bots that had shut down upon being told to do so and the emergency responder bots malfunctioning as they tried not to react to her passing.

And then the little girl in her arms gummed her bot wrist and she understood that all was lost—she felt she was trapped through the baby girl before she had any sense the bot cops closing in.

It's okay.

That was the communication being shared by the child—Neem's last words to her.

Look where you are. It's okay.

Kali looked and saw. She understood Neem's plan in its entirety. His foreknowledge of his death. His foreknowledge of her arrest. Her time in prison with Neem bots that looked like him, but weren't him. He'd known exactly where she would run. Maybe he'd programmed her to run that way. Maybe he'd simply understood her better than she would ever be able to understand herself. Either way, Neem had never intended for himself or Kali to come out of the whole affair safely.

She felt a burning between her legs from all the running she'd done despite not being anywhere near healed from the birth. She felt the sting of betrayal—Neem had sacrificed her for his aims, just as he'd sacrificed himself—but she also felt the peace of understanding each nuanced detail of his plan. The brilliance of what was to come.

Kali finally saw the cops she knew were pursuing her, and with her last few moments as a free citizen, she set her unnamed baby into the mail chute.

NEWER

CHAPTER TWENTY

JOSEPH SIGHED. HE'D BEEN sitting on a bench for a while now, not sure what to do or where to go. Did he want the job he'd been offered? Was he a working man? Someone who woke up every day and put on work clothes? Neem had spoken incessantly about the mail chutes, about the best place to stand and watch them work, so that's where Joseph had gone to think. Joseph supposed they were a bit of a marvel. Drone-free shipping made for less buzzing and with nothing diving down from the sky to drop off packages, people did seem calmer.

People came and went, smiling a little when they met his eyes, not at all seeming to know he was a dangerous criminal let loose on the streets.

Maybe what Neem did really made a difference, Joseph thought. It at least seemed to change the outside of him. Not one person that passed looked at him like he was what he was.

Don't be too pleased, he imagined saying to Neem. He was still a little angry at how their last conversation had gone. He'd thought Neem would at least come to see him off, but the bot hadn't.

The mail chute whirred and then *thwumped,* and there was a package, only it wasn't a package, not really.

It screeched.

"Holy fuck," Joseph said, standing up and crossing the sidewalk, blinking a few extra times to make sure his eyes weren't fucking with him. "Well, hello," he said, picking up the squirming, but silent baby that almost certainly wasn't supposed to be in the mail chute. "What are you doing in there?" He looked at the empty chute to see if there was any hint of how an infant had ended up in the chute in the first place. "I better call someone for you. Eh?" He turned, looking for some clue as to how people on Europa contacted... whoever you were supposed to contact when you found a baby in the mail chute.

The baby gurgled and Joseph's arms felt more comfortable than they'd been in a long time. He'd forgotten the weight of a baby, how little it was, but how important it felt. He looked down again and the baby was looking up at him.

"You're just new, aren't you?" he said. Couldn't have been more than a few weeks old at the most. Did teenagers throw their unwanted babies in the garbage on Europa just like they did on Earth? "Feeling like you didn't get much of a welcome." He snorted. "Don't go thinking that's your fault. Lots of stuff will be your doing, but shit parents just happen sometimes."

Maybe this is how they move babies around up here, Joseph thought. "Should we wait some?" he said to the baby. "Just in case your mom or dad's coming?"

The baby made the same sort of sound that pterodactyls made on the projectors back home. A little groan-screech as she stretched.

Around her neck there was a glimmer and Joseph reached down, turning a very familiar object around in his thick fingers. A metal disk with a dismembered man on it. Joseph couldn't remember the name Neem had given the forgotten god, but he knew this was Neem's talisman. The very one he'd bet when he promised Joseph would be in the right place at the right time.

The baby chomped her little gums down on his knuckle, flooding Joseph's mind with memories of Dani and... something else... not a memory, a request. Neem's gentle voice asking him to deliver the child to the anscestrals, asking him to stay in the woods and watch over the little girl. "There's less porn in the forest, Mr. Lockemore, but far more sex. I expect you'll enjoy yourself."

Joseph snorted and then said, partially to Neem—wherever the bot was—and partially to baby, "Well, I can't argue with that, now can I?"

THANK YOU!
(PLEASE READ)

Dear Reader,

With all my heart, I hope you enjoyed *Newer*. I hope you found a fragment of peace with the time period you're reading in. I hope you're the teeniest bit more open to technological possibilities, aware of the danger and the beauty.

This book was an intense labour of love for me. I was among the first wave of people to lose work to ai and I had to take many steps back to study what was going on in the collective, but also within my own mind and experience, before I felt I could choose how to respond. I'm also obsessed with consciousness and meditation and the beauty of the human experience, which includes creating things that we can't predict all the outcomes of. Children, art, laws, governmental policies, tech—we make things with the intentions we have, and then we watch all the unforeseen consequences of those creations unfold. I don't know how this book will feel in your hands or how this story will feel in your mind, but I made it anyway, in a state of semi-faith that the people who would connect with it would find it somehow.

Thank you for sharing your time and your imagination with me. I've said it before and I'll keep saying it. Stories without readers aren't stories, they're just thoughts written down. YOU are the final ingredient in this tale and any other you choose to let me share with you.

Love,
Robyn

P.S. If this story made you feel anything or wonder about anything, it would mean the world to me if you left a review on Amazon and Goodreads. Reviews are the pulse of an author's career.

P.S. My next release, *Crab & the Blue God,* a folktale from the future, will be hitting shelves and Kindles soon. If you want a bleak-as-fuck fairy tale involving a teenage girl searching for her baby sister in a frozen wasteland full of magic and horrors, this is the book for you. It's one of those, *the future feels more like the past than the present* stories.

ACKNOWLEDGMENTS

So many things help create a book that can't be named. This story was simmering in the back of my mind for years before I wrote it. No doubt conversations I participated in and eavesdropped on have found their way into this story. My interactions with devices, generative ai programs, and algorithms must have shaped the tale somehow. Surely news stories about the state of tech and predictions for the future have also been included.

The help I *am* aware of, however, begins with Floy Joy. Love in the sci-fi package is wild and complicated because we mostly have no idea what world we're living in since things change so fast. Thank you for agreeing to be artists in this feral time with me and for listening to all my theories about that point where tech and consciousness meet, and for all the times someone has brought up ai at a party, and you've looked at me knowing I'm going to say all the weird, hippie things I say.

To Skye, Sydney and Tenaya, #writingbuddies4lyfe, thank you for accepting all the odd stories I throw your way without any warning. You guys make me a better writer, but also a better person.

To Josh Schrei, you don't know me, but experiencing your podcast and seeing how earnestly you share your worldview has been a map for me sharing my own perspectives on things. This book is a part of that.

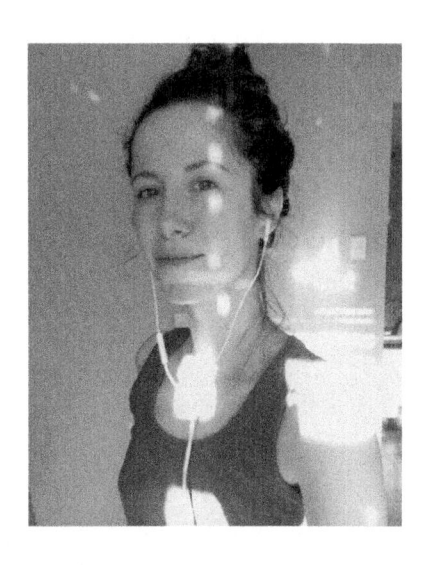

ABOUT THE AUTHOR

Robyn Abbott is a Canadian science-fiction and fantasy author. She writes stories about good people doing bad things. Depending on her mood, she's either a tarot reader or adamantly against tarot reading. Her hobbies include pattern recognition, people watching, and theorizing.

Instagram: @writinginnovember

This is a work of fiction. All names, characters, places, cultures, and events are a product of the author's imagination and are used fictitiously. Any resemblance to real people, alive or dead, or to businesses, companies, events, institutions, or locales is purely coincidental.

Newer

Copyright © 2025 by Robyn Abbott

First edition: February 2024

All rights reserved.

ISBN: 978-1-7389662-3-3

www.robynabbottbooks.com

Editing by
Tenaya MKD
Skye Horn
Sydney Horst

Printed in Great Britain
by Amazon